SPITEFUL
CREATURES

SPITEFUL CREATURES

A.K. KOONCE

TABLE OF CONTENTS

CHAPTER ONE
ALL IN A DAY'S WORK

Aries

Seraphs. They're charming little fuckers, that's for sure.

Just like Zaviar.

"You registered a dirty demon woman. In the realm of the Seraphs and gods. You thought we needed a demon?" The old hag, Mira, spits from over her breakfast.

Careful who you call hag. I'm older than she is. Catherine whispers at the back of my mind.

The slender woman munches delicately on a golden piece of fruit. It glitters faintly against her tongue as she curls her lip at Zaviar and myself. Zaviar stands unflinching in front of me in the little office room.

"She's a Fae," Zav says sternly, a hard line forming between his brows as he folds his arms over his pretty chest.

He can try to look as hard ass as he wants, but he's still a grown man standing in a white loincloth with bright pink wings spanning wide at his back. My bed sheet wrap thingy that a Seraph girl gave me is much more fitting. *Toga.* It's a toga but that feels like a very human thing to call my blessed angelic sheet. It hugs around my inky wings and ties at one shoulder just right. His little scrap of sheet barely covers that bulge, and all it's really doing is emphasizing his beautiful wings that halo over his frowning face.

Speaking of halos. "Will I be getting one of those halos, like in the movies?" I pipe up from my chair in the corner of the crisp white room.

Gods, the lighting in this place. Bliss my ass. Migraine city is what it is.

Mira's golden gaze slides to me like she's just spotted a shit stain on her bleached carpet. She sits her weird apple back down on her white desk.

"Those are called head laces and they're only worn on the day of Celestial." Her lips thin even more if that's possible.

Celestial… right.

"Darine will be in this afternoon. Keep her… busy." She flicks her gold painted nail toward the door and Zaviar follows her unspoken order like some weird toy soldier, marching out with a grenade fitted snugly up his tight ass.

And the moment we're out from beneath the suffocating inspection of the Seraph, I pull the door shut and look up at my brooding guardian angel.

He really has been all this time. *My guardian angel.* He saved me from my own wallowing hell-hole in the Bin and took me home.

I just fuck up all he ever tries to do.

I won't let that happen this time.

"We need to go back," I speak freely for the first time since we arrived here in the Bliss, early this morning.

Yes, Zaviar saved my life. He literally resurrected me. I appreciate it.

But waiting in this anger infected nirvana while my mates and family remain under Corva's reign? I'll pass.

"We can't leave until we've been given an assignment to the Bin. We're low ranking. It takes time." Zaviar's jaw flexes and I'm suddenly aware of how grating this is for him.

He feels just like I do. He's only ever wanted to protect his brother.

Now he's back where he belongs. And too many realms separate them.

The closeness we finally found in the Fae realm is not here now. He's too stressed here. And I really don't blame him.

A sigh that could shake the entire Seraph's kingdom falls from his lips. His eyes close slowly and the memory of how we clung to one another and shared our last breath shivers through my mind. I physically shift in the quiet hall and I suddenly can't look at the beautiful man standing in front of me.

It's pathetic how we do that: we can show so much vulnerability and yet, hide it all away once our thoughts are cleared and defensive. My little brain is practically building up a great wall around my bitch-ass emotions as we speak.

"Let's just get to work for now."

...*work?*

3

"I'm sorry, what?" My guardian angel is sounding a bit insane all of a sudden.

Thou shall not cast unstable stones, the poltergeist at the back of my mind sneers.

The cunt.

Like I said, thou shall not cast cunt stones, she adds.

I blink slowly at her commentary, but try to focus on the real issue here. I push my hair back from my face and brush along the horns curling up from my head.

I focus on glamouring that demonic little trait but something else presses back against my magic… Damn Seraph laws. I don't know them but I know they're preventing me from using the powers I was born with.

Does it affect everyone or just those who don't belong?

"Work?" I repeat as I focus on bigger issue here.

"Yeah," Zaviar motions up the stairs and I follow after his brightly colored wings as we make our way to a much busier corridor just one floor up.

The white tile gleams beneath the hands of two petite Seraphs as they scrub relentlessly at the already gleaming floor. They don't look up at Zaviar and I for even a second. Neither does the white horned woman dusting the marble banister. Nor does the woman who's vigorously polishing knobs in the corner. And no, that's not a euphuism. I fucking wish it was.

Because I'm finally scared. I am shaking in my sheet right now.

"In our down-time we maintain the castle." Zaviar turns to me, and my stomach drops.

No.

SPITEFUL CREATURES

No.

No, no, no, no!

"I—I can't clean, Zav." My eyes are so wide I swear they've spritzed me with something. Intoxicated me with bleach or Lysol or maybe a little Windex to get me in the mood.

He blinks at me a few times. "They'll get you the supplies you need. The fifth floor all the way up to the hundred and third are cleaned daily."

"A hundred and fucking three floors? Zaviar I've never even cleaned *one room*! I'm a fucking Fae princess!" Literally.

His eyes narrow on my scathing outrage.

"Yeah. And right now you're a fuckin' guest." At the sound of his rumbling tone, Slob Knob over there lifts her blonde head our way. Zaviar steps closer to me and doesn't really lower his growling tone but he does get in my face a little. And to think I once bound myself to this ungrateful Seraph. "Clean the halls. Do a good job. And don't draw more attention to yourself than you already have!" He turns dramatically on the heels of his feet and stomps down the stairs, white loin cloth shaking against his ass the whole way.

I linger there, glaring a hole through his broad back until he's out of sight on the fourth floor.

The heavy breath of an overworked Seraph sounds just behind me, and I've never not wanted to face someone so much in my entire life.

"You're the Fae woman," she whispers on a shallow breath.

I can't tell if her tone is filled with admiration or exhaustion from how hard she's been rubbing knobs all morning.

I look back at her. She's cute. Her short soft hair wafts around her chin, big brown eyes peer down on me. She's a couple of inches taller than myself, but still just a tiny little thing.

And small white twirling horns peek out from beneath her hair. I suppose horns aren't abnormal for their kind. Ashen black wings and horns might be but she doesn't comment on that.

"Aries," I say with a sigh. Gods I'm tired already just watching them work. Who can I submit a complaint form to? Is it Mira? Is she HR?

Bliss, I hope not.

"I'm Oliva. I'm headed up to the next floor if you'd want to join me." Her lips quirk just slightly, almost smiling but fuck she's probably too drained to follow-through with the motion.

"Yeah. Sixth floor. Let's do it." I lift my hand with a half assed attempt at pointing toward the stairs at the end of the long white hall, but I'm really contemplating running back and hiding under Zaviar's loincloth all day.

Gods know he probably has some extra space that's not being used.

That's a bald-faced lie…

I sigh and trail after Oliva. My steps are heavy and my heart is heavier.

Every step of the way I wonder if Zaviar should have just let me die.

Because now, he owns me.

Chapter Two

Paint it Red

Aries

Somewhere between the thirty-third floor and forty-seventh, Oliva and I have worked so far ahead of the others that she's started to actually speak.

Freely, I might add.

"You mean they fornicate? With each other?" She's polishing much slower now as she listens to my lovely tales of my time in my home realm, and in the Bin.

"Yeah. All the time. It's a nice pastime."

A shudder runs through her small frame and her thin rag is no longer even moving but just hovering over the crystal doorknob.

"And you've done this… let men just…" Her lips are curled so hard I don't think she'll ever smile again.

"Yeppp," I can't help the smile that's on my lips though. "Sometimes alone, too."

"*ALONE!?*" Her voice echoes all around us within the colorless corridor. "How in the Bin do you do it alone? What are the logistics? What goes in… *there*? And what's the point if the man is not there to force you to make him cum?"

Force me? Oh, my dear sweet knob twirling Olivia. My clit is tsk-tsking this poor girl's innocence while my g-spot's cursing her shit choice in men.

"Well, Liv," I start to explain as I sit cross legged on the floor where I tossed my rag down twenty minutes ago.

"Did I just hear the word *cum* echo down the most established library hall in all the realms?" That disappointed and depressing tone is so familiar to me that I'm already rolling my eyes at him before Zaviar even finishes his scolding sentence.

"I think you're mistaken, and I find it incredibly rude for you to say such a thing in front of Olivia." I stand and brush off my fancy sheet with a pretentious flick of my hand.

Meanwhile, Olivia is now pretending to work, vigorously rubbing her knob so hard I'm sure it's about to spray all over her if she keeps going like that.

I lift my lashes slowly to find Zaviar glaring down at me. His face is smudged with dirt, but the hard lines of disappointment are etched clearly into his features. A solid three seconds that feel like three lifetimes passes as we have our mandatory glare off contest.

I win.

SPITEFUL CREATURES

He looks away and nods his head at me in that alpha way that only he's capable of as he strides off down the hall and down the stairs.

I slowly trail after him, but peer back at Oliva as I pass.

"Bye," I say with a shrug.

"See you tomorrow," she says with a smile and too much cheer.

Tomorrow?

We do this all over again tomorrow?

I'm running to Zaviar then, making it down the stairs and at his side with a heavy sigh.

I should have known.

Tomorrow. And the next day and the next.

Until we're ordered out of here and back to the Bin… and then to my sister's mess.

But…

"Olivia knows nothing of… *dating*," I say that last word like fucking and dating are somewhere on the same scale of life.

They're not. Not at all.

We continue trotting down hall after hall and staircase after staircase. Whiteness. The whiteness is obscene in this joint.

"Seraphs in this part of the realm are careful not to draw attention from those who rule us. We work, keep our heads down and then the very fuckin' moment they let any of us out of our cages, we usually fuck like crazy and find ourselves in more trouble than we can manage. Like getting involved with a possessed Fae." The pretty dark lashes lining his eyes make the look he passes me seem slightly, just slightly endearing.

A smirk pulls at my lips.

"And those who rule us… is that Mira?"

"Fuck, I wish." His pink wings bounce as he picks up his pace on the next set of stairs and I'm a little distracted as I start to pick a few glittering white leaves out of his feathers.

What did he do? Pick a fight with an ostrich over who has the prettier wings?

I mean, obviously he does. Hands down.

"Darine is the head of council. Of the three, Mira is the nicer one of the bunch."

He starts to list off for me, like I'll ever be able to remember all of this.

"Jude is the eldest. Doesn't get involved much anymore but once he's upset he's fucking demonic. But Darine, he's the devil of this realm. Might as well be Krave's daddy for how the bastard acts toward her people."

Hmm they sound charming.

My legs start to tire at the next set of stairs and I've noticed the few Fae who were working are now headed down with us, their shift seemingly ending at whatever hour this must be. They pass us with curious glances, their gazes flicking over Zaviar's wings and then mine. One girl giggles to another, but I make note how her gaze rakes down every ab of Zaviar's chest.

"You have to be careful here. You just—" His lecture gets cut short when his serious look catches someone up ahead.

An old man with long silver hair and a cascading white robe parts the flow of traffic as he walks down the hall. He speaks a catalogue of instructions to Mira and the woman jots down his every word.

And then it hits me.

Jude.

A hand collides hard with my shoulder and the second my back hits the door to my left, it opens and Zaviar shoves me right inside like an avalanche of pure power and... *fear.*

He shoves me hard against the closed door like I'm the lock that will prevent someone from entering. Honestly, with the weight he's putting into my shoulders right now, if someone did try to enter, I'd have a dislocated shoulder and possibly a cracked door jamb to show for it.

"Can you ease the fuck up?" I arch a brow at his seriously constipated features.

He doesn't hear me.

He doesn't even look at me. He looks *through* me.

My hand slides along his wrist and he reacts ever so slowly by releasing the pressure against my shoulders. But he doesn't dare let go.

The sleek white wallpaper closing in around us has a flat white paisley design running along the walls. Wow. They somehow accented white with... white. How very modern of their interior design.

A quaint little desk faces a window that looks out over a snow-white scene of rolling hills. It's all blindingly perfect. Too much so.

My fingertips still linger against his hot skin. His breathing has increased so hard that it blows the long locks of my hair. I think he's listening.

And then I hear it.

"What's this I hear about an unregistered in our realm? Was there or was there not a breach?" A deep voice asks from the other side of the door.

The man speaks slowly, thoughtfully. He asks the question like he has all the time in the world to research this issue.

Fingers flex against my flesh and I soothe Zaviar's blatant anxiety with a brush of my palm up, and then slowly down the veins of his forearms. They're raised and distracting me as much as I'm hoping to distract him. How have I never noticed his veins before? Why are they so masculine to me at this moment? Why in all the realms do I suddenly find that bizarre trait alluring?

Sexy even. God help me.

"Councilman Jude, I've checked the registry several times and all personnel are accounted for. There are no unregistered in our great kingdom." Mira rambles that information out so flawlessly it takes me a moment to realize she's covering for us.

Oh. My. Gods.

Mira is the nice one. What the fuck does that say about the others?

It says I'm fucked is what it says.

"Good! Let's try to keep it that wa—" Their voices fade away into the halls of this palace, as well as into the halls of my anxiety.

My heartbeat is the only thing that fills my ears now. I'm no longer judging Zaviar's broody, moody face. I'm sure my own matches his for once.

I have to live through this realm to make it back to my

own. I have to live to save them.

I have—

"Hey," It's a low timber that shivers right through me. His closeness is suddenly very apparent. The heat of his breath is somehow a warmth against my skin. "I won't let anything happen."

His dark eyes press into me with so much sincerity and even though he didn't say it, I know he means he won't let anything happen *to me*. He's protective beyond reason. He doesn't owe me anything. I literally owe him my life and still he's just worried about saving me even further.

The once restricting hold of his hands along my shoulders is now a caress that slides along my arms. Down my cool flesh, and then he circles those big hands of his fully around my wrists in the most delicate way.

His smooth chest aligns with mine and I lean my head into him without thought. I just need a second. It isn't vulnerability. It's exhaustion.

I'm just so damn exhausted from trying.

I just want a second not to think of all the bad things pressing in around me for once.

During that beat of a second, I fully expect him to step back from this intimacy I'm trusting him with. I imagine he'll step away with a sigh and make an excuse of how we need to do X, Y, and Z before the A, B and C's of this realm come out to get us.

But he doesn't. The stress he held this morning is pressing down on him now. He's my mate again.

Finally.

His hard body is all I feel as he pulls me closer, his big

arms wrapping around me. And then he just holds me.

His palms push back and forth along my back. It's the slowest, sweetest feel of compassion from someone with very little of that to spare

And he's giving it to me.

My fingers that are thoughtlessly held between his chest and mine flex against the hard lines of his body. He's beautifully made. Very much the image of divine creation.

Except for those swirling inky lines along his torso. My nails drag down his abdomen to trace the tattooed letters there but the moment my nails scratch against his flesh, he tenses beneath my touch. His breath stops. The calming movement of his hands against my back halt.

I'm suddenly aware of a bulge pressed low against my stomach.

Oh.

Well then.

I almost step back from him when the heaviness of his palms push lower. I blink and try to let my body react instead of my brain.

Just breathe.

But the air in my lungs is long gone as my very serious angel skims his hands down the high curve of my ass, and then even lower.

And lower.

Until he's gripping me with both hands and the tips of his fingers are so deadly close to the heat between my thighs that I'm trembling in his arms.

No one has that effect on me.

But I'd never expect it from him, either.

SPITEFUL CREATURES

I'd never in two lifetimes imagine he'd be holding me so sensually as a lover. In the realm of the purest monsters in all the lands.

"Zaviar," I whisper breathlessly.

He shifts, but only until his lips hover over my temple. Every breath he takes sends a wave of shivers all along my skin. The rise and fall of my own chest matches his, yet I'm so fucking terrified to move.

Because if I move, if I look up at him, I'll kiss him.

And we'll be even more screwed up in this hellish nirvana than we already are.

Is that what he wants? Does he want me still?

"Don't." His voice is the shadow of a sound. "Don't overthink it, Aries. Gods knows I already have." And then his hands tighten against my ass and in one flawless move he's lifted me.

I'd like to say my legs don't instinctively wrap around his lean hips.

But they do.

They coil around that delicious man like giving out pussy hugs is a common, everyday occurrence for me.

My sheet parts to one side and the warmth of my sex is fully pressed against the rigid outline beneath his thin layer of fabric.

Fuck.

His dark lashes flutter slowly as he blinks at me, his lips are so close to mine that I can taste the trepidation staining his tongue. Dark attention falls to my mouth. The ache in my chest deepens.

We'll ruin everything with a brush of our mouths.

I'll fuck it all up. *Again.*

A faint sound of apprehension slips from my throat but before it fully comes out, his mouth presses ever so slowly to the side of my jaw.

It's a shiver of a kiss against my flesh. It's the briefest of testing moments.

And then he skims that devious mouth of his even lower. His tongue flicks against the curve of my neck over and over again until he's sucking and biting and tormenting me with just a tease of his tongue. The gasp that tears from my throat sets the neediest parts of me into motion. My hips rock into his and he responds so fucking perfectly, he thrusts into me so hard that my want for him doubles. Triples.

It's endless.

My fingers dig into his shoulders while his own trail lower along my curves. His nails bite into my flesh so hard it's like he's trying to part my pussy for the hard outline beneath his sheet.

"Zaviar," I moan. But the thought is lost in my mind as my head hits solidly against the door and I let everything he's giving me fully sink in.

I've never been so wet and so desperate in my entire life.

Because part of me knows, he'll never give himself to me in that way.

Not here.

But I have this. *We* have this single moment of unapologetic rawness.

His shaft grinds into me faster and faster, rubbing hard over my clit in a way that sends waves and waves of pent up energy swirling through my body. It's a demanding but untouchable tightness that doesn't unravel. It just tightens more and more with every thrust of his hips.

It's out of reach.

It'll never come down.

I'll never come down.

The sharp feel of his teeth sinks into my neck just as his thick cock fucks so hard against me I swear I see the stars of this realm.

And then the energy combusts. It shakes through me with sounds of curses and moans screaming from my throat. It's consuming and colliding and I'm just faintly aware of Zaviar's groan joining my own seconds later.

But I'm very, very aware of the wetness that now soaks the pretty sheets we're wearing.

My lashes open partly. I barely get my eyes open from the shining lights behind my lids. When I do, colors assault my sight.

I try to blink it away. The streaming colors of my release fade.

But the bright colors of this room, they're still there.

Confusion kisses the back of my mind before the realization of it all slams into me all at once.

The walls. The paisley white walls.

They're cream now.

The desk. The crisp white desk. It's black now.

And the flawless, virginal white carpet, it's fucking red.

"Oh shit," I whisper.

CHAPTER THREE

A SUMMONING

Aries

"Zaviar," I say for the first time without a hint of lust in my tone.

A grunt is all he gives me, his head now resting against my shoulder as he breathes me in hard.

"Zaviar," I shove at his shoulder and his gaze swings up to mine with a glare that says I should be thanking him for the orgasm instead of yelling at him.

Well. We have bigger problems, my friend.

I nod to the colors splashing through the room behind him. Shit, now the little nameplate on the desk is gold too.

What if it spreads? What if the hall outside of here is now red too?

Fuck. Fuck. Fuck.

His head turns, and I know the moment he sees what I've been gawking at for the past several moments.

"Fuck," he agrees.

His palms against my thighs loosen and ever so slowly he slides me down his chest until my feet touch the now toxic red floor. He steps away from me and assesses every part of our surroundings like it might jump out and attack us.

It may as well.

Get it over with.

A knock sounds softly through the room, but we both jump from the small noise.

Zaviar pushes his palm to the door but it doesn't try to open.

"Aries…" A tiny voice whispers uncertainly on the other side.

Oliva.

Zaviar passes a look my way.

"Yes?" I shift on my feet and I'm just terrified she's about to tell me about a strange color phenomenon happening outside this room.

"I—I thought I heard you screaming. Are you alright?" she asks just as quietly.

Screaming?

Oh… right. Maybe that was me.

"Uh—just thought I saw a terrible smudge on this knob in here. I'm addressing the issue now. I'm fine. Thank you." I close my eyes hard and pray she goes away.

"On the inside. Aries, the office cleaning is designated for elder cleaners. We don't have the training for that!" Her terrified voice stutters from the other side and I can tell I've said the wrong thing. She's just incredibly upset over this smudge situation now.

Zaviar shakes his head with a growl and he's opening the door and shoving me out as fast as he can. I stumble, my sweaty hair flips over my face and the door slams closed behind me before I can even see where I am.

Whiteness. I'm safely back into the whiteness of this fucking place.

Thank the gods.

It didn't spread. It's contained.

Everything's fine.

"What did you spill on yourself?"

I look up at that question to find Olivia's big innocent eyes staring at a spot just below my hips... The cum spot.

Awesome.

Best day ever.

"Uh. Just... nothing." I stare at her. She stares back at me.

"Well. I'm sure Councilman Darine won't notice the extra cleanliness of his knob." She smiles sweetly at me while I vomit at the back of my throat.

"Councilman Darine?"

"Yes. That's his office. He's out for the week, but I'm sure he won't notice that a novice cleaner shined his knob."

The vomit drops back down my stomach and lands with a sickening splat.

It may not stay there for long.

* * *

"Change it back!" I turn on Zaviar the moment he comes down the stairs.

I've been waiting on the first floor landing for nearly an hour.

"I tried." His jaw tics. As does every one of his muscles

as he paces the small space in front of me. "I've never seen that happen here. I've never seen color like that in the Bliss Kingdom."

Well… that's not good.

"Paint? Do they sell paint here? Is there a hardware store we can swing by tonight? Get a flat white and clear all this up before dawn."

His gaze glares through my face so hard I swear I just felt a little burn against my subconscious.

"No, Aries. You're so—" His groan doesn't sound at all like the one he just shared with me upstairs.

My my, how the emotional tables turn with this guy.

"We just need to do what we've been doing."

"Well I think that's what got us into this mess," I cut in and my little input doesn't seem to be helping his emotional temper tantrum.

"We need to keep cleaning and doing as we're told. I'm going to talk with Mira in the morning and see when the next output to the Bin is."

"Can we not go directly to the Fae realm?"

"No. They're a mess. And we're not welcome there. Our kind doesn't deal with them. Too territorial. The human realm is just as pathetic, but they're easier and appreciate our help more," he explains like he didn't just insult me and everyone on the planet in a single breath. "We can only be dispatched to the Bin."

It doesn't matter. I'll get back to Krave, Damien and Ryke either way. I'll stop Corva. I'll fix the mess I've made.

Soon.

"Just come to bed. I'll figure this out in the morning." His exhaustion is tangible. The normal hard line he holds between his shoulders is gone and he just looks like he's carrying too much.

Guilt swallows me whole at that thought.

I didn't even ask how his day was. Is that what orgasm buddies are supposed to do? Ask how the day went?

Why is our relationship such a mess most days?

He guides me through an elaborate hall lined with books on either side from floor to ceiling. The literature is all white bound and colorless, but I make out a few titles here and there. *Dogma. Good Omens. Constantine.* I nearly stumble when I see what's clearly Diana Gabaldon's *Outlander*. It isn't white. It's live and in color.

And I know why.

I pause for a moment and try to remember if there's any angelic link in that one.

Nope. Just incredibly hot, kilt wearing Scotts.

Not even the unearthly divine can ignore a fine man in a good kilt it seems.

Zaviar glances over his shoulder at me and I scurry after the impatient man. I nearly faceplant into his back when he stops and opens a door at the end of the hall.

A door that opens into total darkness.

His hand reaches back and my breath ceases oddly when his fingers lace through mine. With my hand in his, he guides us down the stairs. The shadows are dense and heavy with every landing we stop at before carrying on farther and farther down the endless winding staircase. He checks a door knob that I can't see on every landing, and it seems each one is locked. So we walk on to the next descent into oblivion.

"Where—where are we going, Zaviar?" I ask in a hushed tone that apparently fears the darkness.

"To bed," he answers as he pauses, checks another door, is met with the metallic rejection of a lock, then strides down the set of stairs before stopping at the next level.

"Down here? In this dungeon?" The words barely leave my lips when he starts the process again.

And this time, the door opens.

Light slithers out over the dirty white floor. It's the first time I've seen our surroundings, and I'm suddenly aware of how damp the air is down here. Not to mention the cobwebs that cling to every corner.

But I don't get to look for long. Zaviar leads me into the room and the chatter of a dozen or so Seraphs fill the room.

His warm hand holding mine drops away the moment we step over the threshold of the doorway. His discreteness isn't worth a lot, though. Because though our colorful wings get a few glances here and there in the halls, these people *here* go about their conversations, their laughter, their drinks.

They're at ease down here, hidden away from the prying eyes of their council.

The tension in my own wings falls away at that thought, and I'm suddenly aware of how heavy they've been all day. The edge I've been teetering on since we arrived here no longer feels as sharp and deadly.

There's peace down here.

So much so that I spot a few couples lounging freely against one another. An especially joyful woman near the far wall lies against a dark haired man's bare chest, his arms draping around her like she's the most precious thing in all the realms to him. I don't know why I linger on the pretty blonde's smile. The way she smiles at the things he says, I don't know what it is but it looks like the saddest happiness I've ever laid eyes on.

"I'm grabbing that bed over there," Zaviar says, oblivious to the couple or anyone else really as he makes his

24

way to a small twin bed in the far corner.

I trail after him, listening to the quiet but blissful chatter that fills this space. Even the conversations, the laughter and amusement, it all seems tinged with a faint aria of sorrow. When Zaviar takes the corner bed, I realize the one next to him is free, putting me right next to the loving man and woman I spotted earlier.

Her lips lift just slightly in a kind greeting when I look her way.

"I'm Aries," I tell her. Not to make friends but… to gain information really.

That's what you learn in the Shadow Guard. Casual small talk with strangers is the easiest way to answer unanswered questions.

"Tallin. This is Malike." Neither of them detangle themselves from one another, but they nod lazily my way.

"You're the cutest couple I've ever seen." I plop down on my bed like I'm preparing for girl talk, and even Zaviar is caught off guard by the cheery change in my tone. His dark eyebrow juts high on his broody forehead.

Fuck off, Zev. I'm cheery sometimes. Friendly. Adorable even.

Ask anyone.

"We're not a couple," they both say in unison.

That's what they say, but Malike continues to brush his fingers up and down her bare shoulder while she closes her eyes to the simple feel of his touch.

"Oh. Sorry." I wait for them to feed me information. That's what people do. Though they don't realize it, people love to talk about themselves.

Love it.

…so why aren't they feeding me right now?

Why am I starved and watching their affection like a fucking creep waiting for a show?

"Seraphs don't love in this kingdom, beautiful," Zaviar finally answers before he falls back on his mattress and slides his big arms beneath his head. "It's forbidden. We work. We protect. We honor our kind. We don't fuck. Don't have time for it anyway."

That might be the saddest damn thing I've ever heard anyone say.

A smile tips his lips as he closes his eyes and I can tell he's just so smug to have rendered me speechless.

For a second.

"Your brother makes time for it," I say nonchalantly, peering up at the cobwebbed corners as if I'm not aware of the hard glare he's passing my way right now.

Shit, even Tallin and Malike are prying their puppy-love eyes off one another to double check the words I just said.

"My brother," he emphasizes those two little words like they're speculated hearsay instead of solid factual relation to him. "makes a lot of mistakes." He turns on his side so he faces the wall and doesn't see the hurt anger that's weighting my brow.

A painful strike slices through my chest.

Mistake.

I'm a mistake?

Having me as a mate is a mistake?

Emotions swarm my chest. Thousands of them zap away at my heart and stomach, dipping and diving through me like a sloshing wave at the start of a hurricane.

I can't explain why I do it. I don't even think before I do it and it's doubtful the laws here won't prevent it altogether.

But I guess he's my security blanket in the darkest times

of my life.

He's the one person who never let me feel alone.

And I need him now.

"Krave. Krave. Krave."

"Fuck," I hear Zaviar whisper just before it all happens.

The thin white sheet beneath me shifts, filling with a heated air, wafting up at the center before deflating right back down. The sheet rises once more in a bodily form before wafting to the mattress all over again. Smoke slithers beneath them, hot and heavy. I feel it gather between my thighs before solidifying fully there.

Long black fingers push back the white sheet, and terrifying black orbs look up at me from between my legs. The most gorgeous incubus to ever possess my heart smiles up at me with his messy black hair.

"I do love the way you say my name, Ari" Krave whispers as he clutches my hips in his tattooed hands.

I don't know how, but he's here in the Bliss. The soaring emotions inside me aren't lonely or lost or even hurt any more. They never could be when he's near.

Zaviar's endless curses just make me smile even harder.

"Fuck!"

Fuck is right, my friends.

CHAPTER FOUR
REALM ZERO
Aries

My arms are around his smooth shoulders before I can even take my next breath as his lips are pressing to my collarbone when I finally do find that gasping inhale. And his dick, yeah, his dick is firmly between my thighs, separated only by his black jeans and my white cloth of a gown.

For a moment, I forget about the Bliss, the rulers here, and fuck, even the rules themselves are out the window with Krave tangled up in my arms.

Until he's not.

With a flit of cold air, he's jerked away from me and

lands with a solid thud on the dusty floor.

He leans back on his elbows and makes himself comfortable at Zaviar's feet.

"No," Zaviar scolds like a master to his pup. "Sex is off the table!"

"What about the bed then? Would the bed work better?" Krave asks logically.

"Fuckin' fuck!" Zaviar shoves his hands through his hair and paces the room while the other Seraph's watch with dutiful attention. "How did you even get here? Summonings do not work in the Bliss? What the fuck is happening in my life right now!?" Zaviar spins on his heels and he's stomping right back to the incubus, not even stopping until he's kneeling down, square and level in the demon's face. "What are you? You've always been this shifty piece of shit, but what are you really?"

"Perhaps you should worry about yourself. You're in far more trouble here than I am."

"And why the fuck is that?" Zaviar asks, tilting his head at my sweet little incubus.

"Because--" Krave smiles his haunting amusement at the man. "I can leave the Bliss. And *you*," he stabs a long black sooted finger into Zaviar's solid chest, "*cannot*."

Zaviar's annoyance fades fast, and the worry sinking into his features sinks into me as well. He doesn't look like that self assured Seraph he was just an hour ago.

Why does his false confidence reassure me?

Probably because if Zaviar can't fix this, how the Bliss can I?

* * *

SPITEFUL CREATURES

I've never shined a knob so hard in my life as I am right now. I press my ear harder against the smooth wood of the door. My rag wipes away--nothing, literally nothing--while I eavesdrop intently.

"Zaviar, I told you, when an opportunity comes up, I will fucking assign you. You're a good Seraph." Mira sighs so heavily I can practically feel her breath through the door. "But if you enter my office one more time, I'll exile you to Realm Zero simply for being a pain in my Blissed behind!"

"*Realm Zero!*" Olivia gasps from over my shoulder.

I arch a brow at her shock. The two of us are practically on top of each other's shoulders while we listen.

"What's in Realm Zero?" I whisper.

She shakes her head, her eyes so wide I can only imagine that it's somehow worse than the Bin.

And that's bad.

The incubus at my side pipes up to explain. "Realm Zero is where the Bliss sends their trash to be disposed of. The rebels. The escapees. The Fornicators." Krave's lips twist up in that devious smile of his. "Sounds delightful, really."

"It's not," Olivia says appalled.

"Well, no. Not if you dwell on the torture. But other than that." Krave shrugs and continues to sit his pretentious ass on the sleek white flooring, leaning his back casually against the wall while he watches the stroking swirl of my wrist as I clean... half-ass clean anyway.

After last night, no one other than myself and Olivia notices the dark-horned demon or the glittering wafting magic he swirls in his hands. Whatever magic he holds swirls around him like an electric current. But it hides him, and that's all that matters.

Little glossy hearts keep floating up from his palm and popping like soap bubbles right before his shining black eyes. One pops and another appears.

It seems like he's amused, with a small curve on one side of his lips. But I can tell he's worried. I catch him staring at me like he used to, when he could never have me. Never touch me.

Never love me.

He's afraid.

The two strongest men in my life right now keep hiding their fear from me, and it's just consuming me with terror to even think about our lives.

We're prisoners here.

There's an entire Fae kingdom--my mates included-- who need our help, but we... we may never leave this place. I'm blinking into the dark abyss of that thought when the knob beneath my palm pulls away. I fall forward and a jumble of knees meet my palms. Big thighs and a fine but faint bulge catch my fall beneath my fingertips.

Olivia stumbles without me to support her as well, and I hear the thump of her small frame hitting the ground behind me.

Zaviar's mouth gapes open at us, his head looking back at the councilwoman as he brings the door close to his back and tries to hide my kneeling position from view. Instead of helping me up, he simply slides my ass across the floor like an old mop and pushes me out of the way to close the door firmly behind him. He looks around at the three of us now sprawled across the hall.

SPITEFUL CREATURES

Krave glances up. A heart bubble bursts in his face. He winks at Zav, and the two of them share a passing look of disdain in two completely different ways.

"Mommy said no, huh?" Krave's eyes shine like blazing hellacious stars.

"Fuck off." The Seraph storms down the hall and takes the stairs two at a time.

Dammit.

I drop my rag and follow after him. It's taken about one day for me to realize two things:

1. Seven flights of stairs is my max. Anything more than that and I'll be honest my wings are doing all the work and I'm struggling to give off the appearance that I'm not gasping for air with every step I take.

2. Annddd, holy demon babies is Zaviar in immaculate physical condition. Like bro soars down these steps like they're an escalator possessed by the energizer bunny.

You're possessed too, you know? Put your back into it or whatever it is the kids say. A casual voice says within my mind.

Your back is definitely not what they're referring to in this case, Catherine.

I shake my head and focus on the fluffy pink wings of the man storming ahead of me.

"We need another plan," I say with a hint of breathlessness.

Nah. I'm fine. I'm good.

Damn, did he pick up his pace?

"It's under control," he growls from over his shoulder.

"Seems to me, it's a bit out of control," Krave says as he jogs cheerily at Zaviar's side.

33

I peer over at the cleaners all around us, but none of the Seraph's blink an eye at the incubus here in their domain.

He's completely glamoured. Better than even my magic is capable of, it seems.

How? How can he do his magic but mine is blocked?

"I like the diaper look on you by the way. Your glutes are," Krave makes a kissing motion with his right hand, and that's apparently the straw that broke the brooding Seraph's back.

"I thought I old you to fuck the fuck off!" Zavair stops on the last step and glares up at the towering incubus above him.

Oh... his glamour can't hide Zaviar's outrage though, can it?

Two men hanging a new painting of a crisp white Mona Lisa pause their work to look at the crazy man yelling at... me. It looks like he's yelling at a five-foot-nothing blonde.

Great. Now he just seems like an asshole.

Isn't he? Catherine chirps.

...eh...

"We're fine," I tell the workers to my left with a small-- probably battered woman looking smile. I rush down closer to Zaviar's side and take his arm in mine, ignoring the baiting demon smirking behind me.

I swing Zaviar's big hand in mine and pull him down to the next set of stairs. It's empty, but there are workers both above and below us, so this is as private as we're going to get on the eighty-second floor of the council's kingdom.

"We can figure this out," I whisper, my words echoing through the large space around us.

SPITEFUL CREATURES

I feel the demonic presence at my back before I even turn to him.

"How *did* you get here, Krave?" I look up at him without the interrogating threat Zaviar used as he asked that same question the night before.

His slender shoulders lift in a shrug. "My mate summoned me." His shining gaze tells me there's more to that, but he says nothing else.

My lips part to press him but... it doesn't feel right to order the truth from him. Though we both know that with the bond we share that I absolutely could. It's just... I don't want that between us.

I want him to tell me because he trusts me.

My heart skips a beat of petty worry, but I won't dwell on it.

Not now anyway.

"I'll ask around." I slip past Zaviar and I feel both men watching me as I sway my ass down the stairs with my thin sheet of a gown swooshing in my wake.

"Ask around where? Ask Who? Aries!" Zaviar calls after me.

But, just like the two of them, I have my own ways of doing things.

And those don't always include them.

CHAPTER FIVE

LOVE IS FOR THE LONELY

Aries

The crystal doorknob beneath my palm is cool to the touch, but the sweat clinging to my skin doesn't let me enjoy it much. My wrist turns, the door slips open with a small, careful push. My bare foot steps onto the softest white carpet.

I'm so quiet that all I can hear is my own shaking breath and I halt even that noise to listen. I know I saw her come in here this morning.

But what if she's left? What if someone else is with her?

The three sets of crisp white curtains along the

windows blow in the breeze, slinking over the white desk and chair a few feet away.

Silence clings to the office.

Except... except for a faint humming song coming from a secondary room.

My heartbeat kicks against my ribs, but I don't listen to it as I push the door closed behind me and take slow, soundless steps toward the open door to my right.

"*Fly away, fairy, fly away. Fly away, fairy, far away. Never ever stay*," The woman sings like an--don't say it, Aries. Don't say it.

Like a gods damned angel, okay.

"Pretty song," I say.

She startles so hard she drops the tooth brush in her hand, clattering the little tool to the suds on the floor.

"You... you shouldn't be in here!" Tallin's fingers shake as she picks up the brush once more and gets back to work on the soapy white tile floor. She ignores me, but the tension in her petite shoulders tells me she's still very aware of me too.

She might be nervous, but she's not stupid enough to not finish Councilman Jude's cleaning list.

I close the door of the bathroom firmly behind me with a demanding click of metal sliding through metal.

And only then does she set the brush down and give me her full attention.

"You don't belong here." Her amber eyes narrow on me. "You're something special, but I'm a senior Seraph. Whatever it is you want from me, say it. I have work to finish and a title to maintain."

Damn. I picked the wrong angelic asshole to try to rattle some information out of.

Still. She's telling me how it is and I'd do the same thing if I were her.

"How can I leave the Bliss if I don't belong?"

She blinks silently a few times before answering me directly.

"You can be escorted, of course," she wipes her hands on her apron that's tied around her sheet gown. "That'll get you out of here."

My eyebrow lifts. "To Realm Zero."

Her smug smile and a nod are immediate.

Great.

"That's not an option. What else?" I lean back on the door and fold my arms, fully preparing to be here hashing this out all damn day if I have to.

"You can't. Only those admitted to the Bin by the council are able to exit. If you steal someone's spot or try to sneak in with them, you'll be transported to Realm Zero by default thanks to the protection magic. And escapees are not welcomed kindly in Realm Zero."

"Is anyone really?" I snark before I can stop myself.

Her smile that seemed cruel and telling now appears softer. Genuine and amused.

"Look, I wish I could help you. They'll arrange for you and Private Pink Feathers to go to the Bin. But it could be weeks. Months even."

My mouth falls open so hard I can't even pause to appreciate Zaviar's cute nickname.

"*Months*? I can't stay here that long. I need to go home!"

"Well, calm down, Toto. You'll get there. In time."

I stare at her with my mouth still gaping open. "Toto was the dog," is all I can finally utter.

"Right. Like I said." She starts cleaning the floor once more, and I know the conversation is over. She's dismissed me and it's not even to be cruel. It's because there's nothing left to say.

I close my eyes tightly and very carefully exhale all the pent up emotions pounding on my chest to get out.

When I open my eyes she's looking up at me. She's staring at me with that sadness I saw in her eyes last night.

"You're not the only one, you know. You're not special. Everyone in here is waiting on baited breath to leave. And every one of us dies over and over again when we're pulled right back." Her sadness isn't sorrow. It's acceptance.

That's what she thinks I should do.

Accept it.

My jaw clenches hard.

I fucking refuse.

"Thanks, Tallin." I swing open the bathroom door and the mouse-like steps I walked in here on are not the storming stride I leave with.

I fling open the office door and I sense his dark presence before I collide with his smooth, swirling, tattooed chest.

Krave's strong arms wrap around me in an instant, but I don't need him to coddle me like I did last night.

"What are you?" I ask so loudly the man who's repainting the white wall knocks over his pail of paint.

He curses.

"Oh calm down. It's not like it'll stain," I bark and

immediately wince at my own tone in the silent hall.

I shake my head hard and pull the unseen man down the final flight of stairs. He trots happily behind me as I lead him through the library corridor and to the downstairs door. I jerk the handle and the moment it opens, I shove my demon inside.

"Though I do enjoy the dominant side of you, if you wanted to be alone with me, love, you could have just said so," he rasps as he pulls the door shut behind us, caging me in between his smooth chest and the hard cellar door.

It's cold in the darkness of this space, making his heated breaths feel hotter against my neck. He seems to take his time there, breathing me in, skimming his mouth over the sensitive skin just beneath my ear.

"What can I do for you, my love?" he asks in a tone dripping with sex and sin.

"What. Are. You?" I fold my arms hard, but it only generates a tiny bit more space between myself and his intoxicating body.

Sparkling light strikes within the dense darkness and his magic illuminates the shadows along the angles of his face. And the shining piercing along his lower lip.

Thick lashes shift as he looks up at me from over the faint glinting magic in his palm.

"There are four princes of Hell." Four crowns sketch out and Krave holds them within his palm like he could crush the sparkling image if he wanted to. "They don't mean much, really." He shakes the drawing away but keeps the lights floating between us like glowing fireflies dancing in the dark. "What does it matter to be in succession to be king when your father has ruled for the last thousand millenia?" A crooked smile tilts his lips. "Ever wanted fucked by a royal before? Even a disgraced one like myself?"

My lips part and all that annoyance I had over him keeping a secret from me melts away as my chest warms for him.

He's just like me.

What does a promised crown mean to someone who never intended to wear it? Except... Krave doesn't want it.

I can see it in every single choice he's ever made in his chaotic life.

He just wants love.

I've never really thought about it but Krave... he wants love like some people want fame and money. He's apparently always had the latter.

And now... I want to make sure he never has to look for the former.

"Krave," I whisper, my fingers tangling in his soft inky locks.

He's so close, but he doesn't touch me. His fingertips light with magic, but hover along the curves of my hips as he leans his head lightly against mine. That tragicness he always holds within himself simmers as he closes his eyes and just lets me hold his head in my hands.

"The spark of beautiful magic you always have, it's so dim compared to how you light up my soul," I whisper against his lips. "You found me broken and lost in the Bin, and even then you sparked love like I've never felt inside me."

His eyes close harder and ever so lightly he seems to allow himself the pleasure of touching me. He runs his fingertips softly over my sides, but the pain shadowing his face is still there.

Because he'll never believe that he's worthy of my affection.

And I hate that he and I both know how strongly he believes that.

"Krave," I whisper, closing my eyes once more.

"Hmm?" is his only response.

Maybe his torment is too tight within his chest.

But I'll wash that feeling away. Every. Single. Day.

For the rest of our lives.

"Kiss me like you'll never stop," I command of my sweet incubus.

And he obeys.

His mouth covers mine in a fever of want and desire. The flick of his tongue teases mine and the vague amount of space that I forced between us before is long gone. So far gone that his fingers dig into my thighs as he hikes one of my legs up and positions me just how he needs me to fully feel every single inch of his hardness beneath his jeans.

I missed this. I missed the taste of him. I missed the power he had to crumble away all my worries and just wrap me up in the warm scent of his fiery magic.

My hips barely rock against his, I hardly find any relief to the aching feeling deep in my core when the door behind me pulls out.

And I fall back like a ton of disgraceful bricks.

A quick reaction--not of my own-- saves us. Krave's palm slams to the tile floor and he cradles my ass in one hand and holds us up an inch from the ground with the other.

While I cling to him like a cat dangling from a thin branch.

When I realize no pain is radiating through my body and I'm done thanking a king of Hell for having such a quick-witted son, I'm met with that damn disappointed gaze again.

"Seriously if you could stop being so fucking dramatic when you open doors, you wouldn't find me falling at your feet all the time," I tell Zaviar before he has a chance to utter a single angry word at me.

"Notice anything about the cellar door, beautiful?" The Seraph folds his big arms across his chest and his arrogance alone tells me I don't want to even look.

But I do.

And it's worse than I could have imagined.

Instead of a fresh red door like I expected from Krave and I's little sinful lust fest... There's just a splotch of red in the middle... not a splotch exactly... more like a…

"Is that your ass print, love?" Krave asks curiously.

I *hate* that he's right.

Fuck!

CHAPTER SIX

LEAVE

Aries

I think about the splashes of red I've left around this castle and how little time it has taken for me to taint its "perfection". This entire fucking realm will be crimson if I'm here for a month.

And who knows what kind of havoc the Fae realm is suffering.

I peer over at the incubus sitting at my side on my tiny mattress. Krave's head is tipped back and his eyes are closed. The light of the room reflects off of his metal piercings as well as sharpens the hard lines of his jaw, his throat, and his collar bones.

He looks peaceful as he rests. As much as I want to ask him about Ryke and Damien, I can't bear to disrupt that calm that's spread across his features.

"Either ask the question or kiss me, love. The staring is bordering on the creepy side at this point," Krave says quietly beneath his breath.

A smirk pushes at my lips as I continue to watch him rest, never once peeking open a dark eye to look my way.

But he knows me too well.

"Has Corva done anything yet? Is everyone okay back home?" My voice is steady despite how hard my heart pounds to know the answers to the hundreds of questions in my mind.

"The night it happened, Ryke stayed with your mother. He protected her like you asked. Damien was the first to notice you were gone. That both of you were gone. Amid the chaos, we searched for you two, dodging the bloody Pixies and the magic that lashed out at us around every corner. But when we couldn't find you," Krave opens his eyes then and studies the darkness of the ceiling, "We searched for your mother. As twisted as your relationship had always been with her, I just thought you'd have gone to her in your final hours. A mother's love may seem like nothing to some. But in the end, it's *everything*." A shiver shakes through me. "So we went to the Queen first. But you weren't there. I—I honestly have no idea what Corva's done after that night. Because the four of us have been searching for you ever since then."

My heart pivots and dives.

"Four?" I blink at him for a long, long moment.

"Your mother left the castle. She went to the Shadow Guard immediately, and the four of us along with so many of them, we searched for the missing Princess of Roses."

SPITEFUL CREATURES

The feelings inside me are a well so deep I never realized how bottomless it really was.

My mother left her people to find me.

My mates did the same.

Even the Shadow Guard who hated me for my recklessness, they came looking for me.

"The Shadow Guard has your mother and friends in an abandoned cottage north of the river." His warm hand slides over mine. "They're fine, love. Everyone's fine." His eyes narrow, and a thought appears to literally pass over his features. "Well, not *everyone*. I have no idea what's happening to the people of your kingdom. They might not be in the best shape, really." His head bobs back and forth in a nonchalant kind of tilt causing the anxiety within me to rear right back up.

Of course they're not fine. Fuck. Fuck. Fuck.

"Krave," I say on a trembling breath. "I need you to go. I need you to go back."

His hold on the back of my hand tightens, but he doesn't interrupt me.

"Go back and distract Corva until I can get there. Try to help the people there the best you can until I can join them."

He swallows so hard I can see the tension of his throat as he continues to just let me say my peace. I almost think he'll argue, or try talking me out of it.

I wait for it, actually.

"If that's what you need me to do, then I'll do it. Send me where you need me. I'll always find my way back to my princess." His gaze shines as he looks at me, and I swear in this moment that my heart beats just for him.

It aches just for him.

47

I nod solemnly.

"Leave me," I whisper as I have so many times in the past. But this time it hurts. This time I hold on to him so tightly I hope the magic of my words don't work.

But I know they will.

"Leave me."

His eyes close with the most pained expression lining his features.

My lips press to his with a soft kiss and he leans into the feel of it. Even as I whisper against his mouth once more, "Leave me."

An ashen smell tinged with a hint of cinnamon lingers in the air. His warmth still taints my skin and I cling to that sensation, eyes clenched shut, heart hurting so bad I think it might literally break.

He's gone.

It isn't forever. It's not.

But it feels like it is. Everything right now feels so damn permanent. My life feels permanent.

And empty.

The mattress dips beneath me and I open my eyes to the sweetest look this man might ever possess in his entire miserable life. Zaviar's hand hesitantly slips around my waist and without even questioning it, he pulls me hard against him. I don't question it either. I accept his comfort for all that he has to give. He holds me against his chest and my hand slips around his smooth abdomen to bring him as close as possible. Until all I feel and all I breathe is the strongest, sweetest, asshole-iest Seraph the gods ever created.

He shifts, so I follow his movements as he lies back

against the bed. I curl into every part of him and he lets me. He protects me from the thoughts inside my own head.

He protects me.

And I love him for it.

CHAPTER SEVEN
TEMPTATION AND TORMENT

Zaviar

I've never felt so invincible and so vulnerable at the same damn time.

That's what this psychotic woman does to me. She baits me and harasses me and chips away at my own walls just to let her climb right inside my heart itself.

That's where she's living right now as she nuzzles her nose into my neck and I try my fuckin' best not to take things sexually in this bizarre moment we're sharing. She's finally asleep.

Fucking finally.

She makes little restless noises even while she rests. She can't even shut up while unconscious.

Even I have to admit that it's cute.

Dammit.

In the candle light of the night, I feel someone watching us. I know we're safe here in the cellar of the castle. The council could never bear the thought of venturing down here themselves. But still… someone's watching.

My gaze flicks open and the blonde that sleeps next to Aries has her big eyes on us. I can't decipher her look. Is it a "they're adorable" look, or is that a Im-gonna-run-right-to-Mira-first-thing-in-the-morning-and-fuck-your-life-all-up look?

"She needs you," the blonde finally whispers.

My eyes narrow on her before my eyebrow slowly lifts.

The last thing Aries Sinclaire would ever need in her life is me.

"She needs someone rational to pull her back when her plots and her own thoughts threaten to swallow her whole. Trust me, she needs you." She gives us one more lingering look, and then rolls over to slip into the arms of the man she's always leaning into.

I study the two of them for a long moment in the dim lighting. Even in his sleep the man instinctively holds her close…

What the fuck does she know about Aries and I?

Nothing.

She doesn't know shit.

Nosey fuckin' Seraphs. I absolutely hate this place.

Aries exhales a little moan against my throat as if she's agreeing, but my cock seems to think it's a different conversation. That's not the discussion. That. Is. Not. The.

Discussion.

I close my eyes and force myself to just enjoy holding her. It's nice really. The two of us never just silently exist together. There's always conflict and bickering.

But this… it's kind of nice taking care of her.

For once.

My arms loosen around her slight frame. I relax into her just as she's relaxed into me. My thoughts shut off. My body shuts off.

Then sleep begins to play at the edges of my mind.

"Zaviar." The voice is far off, but I hear it.

And I recognize it so fast it claws at me, digs its nails in and yanks me from the caresses of sleep.

Because that's what monsters do. They fuckin' haunt you mind body and soul.

The breath in my lungs staggers. My eyes fly open. A long willowy man stands above me, here in the cellar where no Council member has ever stood.

It must be bad fuckin' news for Darine to be here.

And it is.

"My office is splattered blood red," he tells me in that droning tone of his. Nothing ever excites him.

Nothing.

Except for torment.

The slow smile that carves across his thin features tells me that it's torment that's in his eyes right now.

My hold on Aries tightens a little harder. I wish I could protect her. I tried to from the very start.

Now it's too late.

CHAPTER EIGHT
WITHOUT REMORSE

Aries

A pain, like flesh peeling away to reveal the muscle and bone and blood underneath slices through me so hard I scream myself awake. The feel of it is still trembling through me as I hug my arms around myself on the broken glass floor... That's what it is. The floor's made entirely of mismatched, bloodied and jagged shards of glass. In the dim lighting, spots of blue sea and crimson stained glass lie in piles along the floor like a gruesome work of art.

I try not to shift against the discomfort beneath my thighs. The strength I put into clenching my jaw shut is enough to make my eyes water.

But I show no weakness.

Especially as a wickedly smiling tall man stars down at me from a far too close proximity.

"Where--where am I?" I ask on a pitifully shaking breath.

The crunch of glass is such a nasty sound that it feels like it's raking into my very bones as he strides around me in a slow, prowling circle. He feels no pain because his feet… are hooves. They're as white as the horns spiraling up on his head. They're the same color as the angelic wings along his back.

"You're in Realm Zero. You didn't really think we'd let a trespassing Fae go under our radar for as long as you have, did you?" His steady voice rumbles with humor and smugness.

"And yet, I did stay in your pretentious little realm for as long as I did. Didn't I?" I tilt my chin up at him and he stops before me, his lips pulling down hard at the corners.

The speechless fuck.

The defined bones of the back of his slender hand strike down hard and fast across my face. The blow stings into me so fast that when I react, it only causes me to cut myself deeper on the bed of glass beneath me.

A cutting cry scatters from my throat before I can stop it.

"Aries!" A familiar voice calls out to me.

The rumbling tone is a warm memory. But that memory is tainted with the sound of weakness kissing his voice.

"Zav..." With my fingers still pressing to the blood sliding down my chin I search for him. I look up at the edges of the room, but it's dark and dim and shapeless aside from the faint spotlight around me. "Zaviar!?" I all but yell for him.

Fuck this angelic asshole.

SPITEFUL CREATURES

I push down as much as I can bear and prepare to spread my wings wide and soar above all the pain to find him. But when I extend my wings, they don't move. The inky feathers at my back rustle, but a hold is wrapped tightly around the most delicate, beautiful part of me.

Barbed wire is spun like gold over and over and over again around them, and it's only then do the tears in my eyes slide silently down my cheeks. They want me to suffer.

This is the start of it.

"What will you do to me?" I ask so quietly it's just a dry rasp of words.

The man lowers himself down, balancing on his strange hunches as he stares at me with a disgusting glint in his hateful glare. The driest palm drags down my jaw as he forces me to fully look him in his ice-blue eyes.

"I'm going to do to you what I've already done to Zaviar." The pleasure on his face causes acid to burn up my throat and kiss the back of my tongue. "I'm going to strip you naked. I'm going to reveal you in all your blessed glory. I'm going to take that flawless skin of yours and turn it into layers of thick scars. I'm going to pluck your pretty feathers one by one until a downy of comfort blankets this broken glass floor." His smirk is jagged cruelty. "And then I'm going to saw those blasphemous wings off your nasty body and burn them right before your very eyes before I slit your throat so shallowly that the fire will burn out before you ever get the chance to bleed dry."

What. The. Fuck is wrong with this guy?

How could I ever think Krave was a creature of evil now that I've met Psycho Mcgee over here?

One thing does linger in my mind.

Zaviar... I think back to the way he called out my name. It was breathless and pained.

But it wasn't a shallow throat slitting pain.

"You're lying." I hold his gaze and I nearly want to look away simply from the manic shine in his eyes.

"I am not, my pretty princess."

"Then torment me some more. Show me my friend."

My mate.

He's been bonded to me all along and all we could do for the last several days was shove all our anger and anxiety into each other.

And now we're here. In the worst realm I've ever stepped foot in and I've taken a tour of Hell for fuck's sake. The Torch has nothing on Realm Zero.

"You mean your lover?" His arrogance is really beaming now. Even as my eyebrows pull together hard at the word lover. "Yes. I'm very aware Zaviar snuck you into the Bliss, and I'm very aware you two tainted my office with your... *fornication*," he hisses that last word and a visibly disgusted shiver races through his frame as he stands and dusts off his hands. Like my *fornication* has dirtied his desperately in need of Aveeno hands.

"Show him to me," I demand instead of correcting him.

His large white wings flutter as he straightens his stance to his full and abnormally slender height. With a wave of his long fingers, a cage swings forward. It slices down like a pendulum and sways back and forth in the same manner. The black bars shadow across its occupant, but it doesn't stop me from seeing the man lying in a puddle of blood.

The pink feathers of his wings are still visable and still

very much attached but the torture the councilman described has clearly been started. Those beautiful scrawls of latin across his ribs are no longer legible. A mixture of dried and fresh blood drips from the thousands of cuts sliced across his bronze flesh. His beautiful body is nothing more than deep lines of muscle tissue jaggedly etched over every available inch.

Including his god-like features.

The gasp that leaves my lungs sounds at the same time as the meaning of his tattoos resound in my mind.

Without Remorse. Without Forgiveness.

It makes sense now. The tattoo never fit for an angel.

But a Seraph and an angel are not the same thing. And this cruel councilman, he's driven that point deep inside me now.

They live without remorse and without forgiveness.

And I'm going to kill this motherfucker in the same way.

As he turns to admire his handiwork, my bare feet press into the glass with force. My body extends fully.

We collide in a flash of resilience.

And I hurtle his smug ass to the floor. The satin wrap covering most of his body rips on contact as his back hits the tiny slivers of glass. His groan of discomfort is so pleasing that I no longer feel the pain all along my thighs or feet. I smile even. I smile as maniacally as he smiled at me just moments ago.

"How's it feel?" I ask as my palm plants into his cheek and shove one side of his face into the serrated floor. "Feels good, huh?"

"*Aries,*" Zaviar whispers.

That single sound of his voice pulls my attention right

to him. The cage above doesn't move an inch now as he lies there, his bruised and swollen face staring out at me from between the bars. "Just kill him," he tells me with a pleading groan.

Right.

Right. I need to get on with it. People are suffering. Now is not the time for slow vengeance.

When I look back at the man beneath me, his wings clatter against the glass as he spreads them wide, soaring up so fast I'm flung down to the ground. My shoulder hits hard from the few feet of incline the fucker got. Biting pain stabs into me and I barely give myself time to breath out the feel of it before I'm searching him out.

But only darkness and hazy edges of the room are visible to me.

"What's wrong? Don't like to play?" I ask him as I hug my bloody shoulder with one arm.

His echoing chuckle is his only response at first.

"On the contrary," he says in a breezy whisper that flutters around the room from all angles.

My gaze never stops shifting. Every muscle in my body is tense and ready.

He darts out with a blow that pins me down like a beaten moth. I wasn't ready for that. His nails bite into my wrists, his legs are crushing mine while the slices beneath my back and wings just cuts in deeper and deeper.

A scream I can't contain crawls up my throat and as my lips tremble, he leans in closer. And closer. And closer.

The tip of his pink tongue slips out and the wetness of it slides over my lower lip, along my jaw and across my neck.

SPITEFUL CREATURES

My leg jars to bring my knee up, but he's too powerful. He holds me down with more strength than I've ever felt.

How old is his magic?

"You're going to be *delectable*," he whispers in my ear on a heavy, pressing breath.

And then a sharpness cuts into my flesh where his tongue once was. It cuts into me, and the warmth of my own blood gushes down my throat.

My arms jerk back and forth, but it's no use.

Even as he makes his next slice just below the first.

His sickly breath hits my skin just before the pain of the slicing sensation cuts into me.

…It's his teeth.

The slices and the scars he's promised me, he's going to etch them into my flesh with nothing more than his mouth.

I scream as the next wave of misery washes over me just beneath the other wounds and though I can't move my arms or legs, I'd never let a fucker like him hurt me without a fight.

My jaw clenches and with as much strength as I can manage, I fling my head sideways into his. The crack of his skull hits mine with too much force. Black spots flash over my vision and his curses are all I can focus on.

That… and he's released one of my hands.

My fingers bite into my palm and I don't aim for his blood covered mouth.

No, I aim to maim, not to hurt. The full force of my knuckles lands hard into his throat.

The immediate reaction of his gasping and coughing is music to my ears as I roll across the jagged glass to escape him. The sticky cuts and blood covering my body are endless. I feel the pain of every one of them as a single sore that aches down to my bones.

And still I shove myself up off the slicing ground and limp my way over to the man taking harsh little inhales and rasping, raking exhales.

My foot braces as I bring the other one back and sail it forward with all my might. The smack of his jaw from the impact is a pleasing sound. So much so that I do it again. And again.

Until the top of my foot hurts and I too am out of breath. His palm reaches up for me as his bloody face turns my way.

"You'll—you'll regret this," he rasps.

Maybe. Maybe someday I will.

But right now, it feels so fucking good.

A flicker of the mysterious dim lights flash low with a humming volt of electricity.

Smoke wafts through the room.

And a tall silhouette forms from a few feet away.

My heart drops.

I'm too battered to fight another council member right now.

Seems he was right… I might regret this.

My wings strain against their prickly bindings, but I still can't fly my way out of this.

The crunch of glass resounds through the room with every step that the man takes closer and closer to me. It grinds right into the quick beating of my heart. My nerves kick up as he steps into the minimal lighting.

And beautiful black eyes meet mine.

"What did he do to you, love?" Krave whispers, his long fingers trailing delicately along the bloody sides of my face.

Krave's gaze drops to the beaten and bloody Seraph on the floor. His features harden as he looks at the man who hurt me. His attention stays pinned to the councilman while he wraps his arm beneath my legs and the other around my back. He lifts me against this smooth chest as he continues to consider the man at his feet.

"The space between this realm and the Torch is just a hop and skip. They should get better security here like we have in the Torch. Any demon with high enough authority could stroll right into this dump." Krave takes a step forward and I note that his boot lands firmly on the delicate white wing of the Seraph.

His wavering scream is a comforting sound while I simply rest my head on Krave's shoulder. My eyes close and the melody of his pain calms me.

He can't hurt us now.

Krave's here.

"I'd kill you, but your kind just comes right back, don't they? Like crazy ex's, or cockroaches," Krave muses. He takes another step and I hear bones break this time.

More chaotic pain trembles from the councilman's lips.

Krave takes a tiptoeing jump over the man as if he doesn't want to accidentally hurt a hand or arm, but from the bouncing way he lands and the sharp cry of utter agony tells me, he landed firmly on the other wing. The demon gives a happy wiggle of his hips, then hopscotches right along for a bit longer on Darine's bones and feathers.

And then he walks away.

He heads into the shadows and I hear him clank against something metal. My eyes open just in time to see my sweet incubus reach for Zaviar. Zaviar's bloody hand fumbles as he clasps palms with Krave. There's a shared look between them. A look of total understanding and trust that I've only ever seen Zaviar give one other person.

His brother.

My arms hold Krave a little harder. My head nuzzles into the warmth of his neck as smoke slithers around us in the scent of charcoal and cinnamon. My eyes close gently as the room fades away completely and I just know.

Everything's going to be alright.

For now.

CHAPTER NINE

LOVE

Aries

Peace is the most undervalued substance in the world. It's the greatest high we never acknowledge. And we never realize it truly exists until we've been broken down to the barest form of ourselves.

It's there.

I feel it washing in like a cleansing sea, sweeping into every fiber of my being right now.

Until…

"Aries, please. Please wake up," a soft voice whispers.

Cold fingers brush through my hair and all that peace I found is *fucking gone*.

A groan that shivers deep inside wakes me, and I wish it

hadn't.

Gods, just let me die.

"Aries!" The woman gasps.

My lashes lift, dry eyes meet the warm sunlight that's beaming into the room and her wet, shining eyes are the first thing I see.

"Mom," I rattle on a shallow voice.

An unsteady smile pulls at her lips and she's never in my life hovered over me so closely before.

Especially not since Nathiale.

"I was worried you'd never awaken." Her hands no longer stroke my hair, but she continues to hold my head in her icy hands as if she'll forever protect my skull just like this for as long as I walk these deadly realms.

"I'm fine," I tell her, holding back the wince as I shift the slightest bit beneath the blanket.

I peer around then at the small cottage style bedroom.

"Where are we?"

"Your Grandmother's secret cottage." She reaches for a glass on the side table and brings it to my lips.

I stare blankly at her for a second before tilting up just enough for cold water to touch my lips. I only take a sip at first. And then I push forward for more. I drink until the cup's empty, and still my throat feels like fire has crept down it in the middle of the night.

She pulls away and puts the cup down with a careless rattle before she's right back to helping me lie on the fluffy white pillow.

It's soft, and the bed is warm.

SPITEFUL CREATURES

And… this place is a beautiful secret.

"She had a secret cottage away from the one they built for her?" I digest that it only makes me fonder of the eccentric woman I've only met once in my life.

My mother nods.

"Damien and Ryke, are they here?" I cling to her silence until she finally nods once more. But that doesn't ease the tension in my chest. "And Zaviar, how's he?"

Once more I'm hanging on her every move, but she doesn't reassure me. Instead she looks to the door. She doesn't meet my eyes.

"He's—he's healing. Just like you. Scarred more than you, though." Her gaze pauses on the side of my face… where three painful wounds sting along my jaw. "It's taking more time for him." Her fingers toy with one another in her lap and just as quickly as she'd fussed over me, she stands.

Her pale hands smooth her fine gown as she collects that impossibly regal stance of hers. Her spine is so straight it seems like she's never bowed before anyone in all her life.

She's the Queen of Roses.

And she's been driven out of her castle.

"Will you send Ryke in?" I ask, because I know she's about to leave me.

She isn't good at mothering.

My father never let her be.

She was his source of power. Nothing more.

And that has bent our relationship.

"He's been waiting at the door for the last three days," she says with a sweet smile.

67

…she… she likes him, I think. Does she approve of my mates?

"The incubus keeps swirling portraits of you in his hands. At first, I thought it was merely a doting love, but sometimes they're erotic and just not at all what a mother wants to see. Especially right now." Her lips curl hard, and I have to force myself not to smirk.

I suppose she doesn't approve of all of my mates…

I can't really argue and say that *dead* ol' Dad liked Krave. That's not an endorsement at all. I simply don't care. Because I know Krave is good. Deep down in his dark little core, he's the kindest demon Hell ever spit out.

He's the most loyal *man* I've ever met.

She slips from the room and before the door closes, a big palm is pushing it back open. And broad shoulders and pure deadly strength comes rushing into the little room.

Ryke collapses over me, blanketing me entirely with the protection of his body.

"*Aries,*" he whispers like my name itself is a sacred prayer.

His head leans into my abdomen and his big hands wrap fully around my waist as he just absorbs my presence. My fingers brush over his hair, his beard, the smoothness of his shoulders and the warmth of his black leather wings.

Being in the Bliss for so long, I think I forgot what a truly beautiful Seraph looked like. Especially a fallen one like Ryke.

He's perfect.

So, so perfect. Powerful and loving all at the same time.

"…Ryke," I say slowly.

SPITEFUL CREATURES

He never looks up at me. He just holds me.

Even as I whisper the most gentle words I've ever said to him, "Ryke, I love you so much. I never want another day to slip between us without telling you how incredibly important you've always been to me." I blurt the words out fast and tangled and the pressure in my chest feels like this moment is the only moment I'll ever have to tell him and even saying it now doesn't compare to the heart echoing feelings he brings to me.

He doesn't lift his head to my urgent confession. He holds me with a crushing hug around my torso and it almost seems to pain him to hear it all laid out like that.

But still he doesn't respond. He doesn't even open his tightly clenched eyes.

"Ryke… did you hear me?" I finally ask, though I know from the pinched expression on his face he did. "If you—if you don't feel that way about me, I'll understand. It's just I needed to say—"

"Of course I feel that way! Just looking at you makes me feel that way, beautiful."

"Then why do you look so tormented about it?"

The lines creasing his face soften, but only just so. "Because. Shit, look at me, Aries," he pulls back from me and his head tips up, but his gaze still lingers so far away from mine. "I never really thought it could be like this. I don't deserve this. I definitely don't deserve you. Never mind the family you've built around me with Damien and the others." The way he shoves his hand so harshly through his short, dark hair looks painful, like he's hurting himself with the simple gesture.

If I thought my heart pounded for him before, it's breaking for him now. That's what he does: he gives me heart aches and heart breaks. It's funny how similar they feel, one right after the other.

I lift, and the stabbing sensation that overcomes me is a vague wince that I don't acknowledge. I slide my fingers up the bulging muscles of his arms and tenderly take his face in my palms. The coarseness of his beard kisses my skin. The ruggedness of his features tingles in waves through my body. The pure demonic-ness of his overall being is a warmth he would never understand if I could explain it.

Hell, even I don't understand it.

But he feeds me these emotions like I'm starved.

And yet, he feels unworthy of the love I try to nourish him with.

"Ryke," My hair brushes his as I lean so close to him he breathes me in.

"Let me love you," I whisper.

His lashes close once more, their lines fanning around his beautiful eyes. It's that same pained expression. It hurts me far more than any damage the Bliss did to me.

"I'm going to love you whether you let me or not. But I promise it'll feel better if you just accept it."

"I love it," he rumbles like it's a real discomfort for him to admit.

"Do you?" My eyebrow arches high as a smile tips my lips.

"Yes," he grimaces.

Another unconvinced look is all I'm capable of.

"Because I love you too, beautiful," he says in the worn-out tone of a man who's finally coming to terms with what's out of his control.

That's our love: Entirely out of control.

In the best possible way.

His lips press like a breeze against my lips and I'm leaning into him for more, even with the groan of pain that's caught in my throat from how much (or how little) I'm moving.

He pulls back just enough to leave my breathlessness between us.

"Get some rest. Zav's been asking about you." He still holds me loosely, but somewhat like he's about to go.

And his words have me nearly following after him before he's even gone.

"Zav? Is he really alright?" A thousand and one terrible things slam through my mind all at once.

"Yeah." Hesitation presses against the walls of the room.

"Yeah?" I pull back to really stare him in the face.

"He's fine." It's then that he does stand, fully disengaging himself from my desperately scanning eyes. "Rest."

"I want to see him."

"Tomorrow."

"No. I'm fine. I want to see him tonight."

"Aries," Ryke's stern look is nothing compared to my heated glare. "Lie your ass down and rest. You know that Seraph's too damn stubborn to die. And he's especially too stubborn not to see you. Which is exactly what he's doing. Because he knows you need your rest. Just like he does."

I think thorugh that back and forth fuck-all of logic.

"Fine." I lower myself back into the soft pillow with a small grimace as jabbing pain cuts through the underside of my legs and back.

He lifts a cup to my lips once more. The one I'd emptied earlier.

The liquid is cold and refreshing against my tongue and I swallow it down as fast as I can. He lowers the cup and I lick the dampness from my lips.

It tastes acidic… strange…

Suspicious.

"Ryke?" I ask through a blinking haze. "You drugged me!"

A smile pulls at his lips. "It's called medicine. It'll heal you. And yeah, it'll force you to fucking rest."

My eyes close heavily as a soft kiss presses to my temple. "I love you. So damn much, Aries," he whispers in a far off voice.

My lips open to say it back…. Or possibly to curse his ass out.

But nothing comes out except for even and satisfied breaths.

And then I rest.

CHAPTER TEN

SAVE HIM

Aries

The night falls in the blink of a drugged out eye.

Warmth wraps around me and the hardness of a chest from behind has me wiggling into the man who is curled so perfectly around my body.

It's the softness of his touch that gives him away. The warmth, but the wanting of his hands.

"*Damien*," I murmur, still half asleep.

"Shh," he whispers.

The gentle way he encircles me in his embrace is everything I never knew I needed in life.

I turn swiftly beneath the blankets and find those sweet

brown eyes looking down on me. "I missed you so fucking much," he confesses, his hand sliding back and forth along the smooth skin between my wings. He massages there just right.

It doesn't hurt any more.

Whatever Fae or goblin magic was in that medicine has a rapid reaction it seems.

"You've slept for four days. I've wanted to see your eyes open so damn bad."

"Four days!?" I repeat, already shoving out from beneath the now constricting blankets.

His hands fall down the length of my arms, fingers caressing but not holding me back as I slip away from him.

Jeans and a white tee-shirt are folded neatly in a chair next to the door. The thin gown that's tied behind my neck falls away with a pull of the silky string. Cool night air wafts over my stomach and breasts, and I hear the shifting of blankets as I begin to unfold the jeans.

The blankets were a faint sound. The steps he took to cross the room, those were soundless.

Rough palms brush over my hips and I halt in his hands as his fingers press slowly into my skin, one by one. My jeans are snug and stay around my thighs as I abandon them to hold on to him as much as he holds on to me. There's a perfect smoothness to how his chest melds against my back, my wings fluttering just slightly out to ensure he's nuzzled nicely against me. The hard pounding of his heart storms through my own chest and I just close my eyes and focus on the steadiness of his breath along my neck.

"So fucking much," he repeats like a prayer.

I missed him too.

SPITEFUL CREATURES

I craved to know he was safe. But I selfishly craved the feel of his skin against mine just as much.

Every single fucked-up thing in the entire realm seems so meaningless when he touches me. That's what he does to me: he lets me forget.

For just a little while.

The skimming of his lips along the lowest part of my neck sends a shiver running through my chest, my core, my legs.

"Come," he whispers between kisses, and my sex instinctively reacts as I shift against him.

But a smile curves his lips as he rakes his teeth against my skin. "I meant come with me." A rumble of laughter shakes through him while confusion still lingers in my lust-filled thoughts.

The white shirt is in his hands before I understand, then he's helping my wings through it and covering me without an explanation. In fact, I'm still shimmying into my jeans when he opens the door.

I barely have the button done when he slips his hand into mine and guides me into the darkness of the little cottage. The shadows drift in the moonlight shining through a big bay window that frames the beautiful river just outside.

The house is so similar to Hyval's that it makes me realize how much she must love the sound of running water. Does it calm her messy mind?

It does for mine.

I'm still looking out at the long vines dipping into the gushing river when Damien pulls me away toward a little hall with two doors on either side. Not even the quiet sound of a turning knob can be heard as he pushes the door slowly open. His broad shoulders blend into the darkness of the open room and I find myself leaning closer to my fallen angel.

Until he steps aside, and the broken body of Zaviar lies before me.

A gasp tears from my lungs as I brush past Damien and fall to the floor in front of the little bed in the corner of the small room.

My hands shake and my fingers seem cold as I press them to the deep lines ripping over his tragically handsome face. Heat swells off of the hundreds of fresh scars. His soot colored lashes flutter, a groan and a wince follows as I touch him ever so lightly.

I bring my hand back instantly, fingers still trembling as I hover there over his bruised features. The stern lines I'd grown so used to between his brows are gone. They're replaced with jagged flesh.

I don't know why, but the first time I saw him walk into that mansion in the Bin flashes through my mind. The hardness of his beauty was apparent. It was the confidence of a man who could give as good as he got.

He's a battered reflection of that man now.

Because of me.

A drop of wetness falls to his forehead, and it's only then that I realize I'm crying. A sniffle sneaks out and I shove the tears away rather roughly before standing.

"He's woken up a few times. We keep feeding him the medicine your mother gave us. But…" Those quiet words slip away when he shakes his head hard. His jaw is clenched just as hard. Anger and worry press against the brow of Damien's features and I know he feels the exact same way I do at this moment.

Without Remorse.

Without Forgiveness.

There will be no fucking forgiveness for what Darine did.

* * *

I don't wait for the sun to dawn. I rush into the room across the hall and despite my determined rage, I stop in my tracks when I find a beautiful man making friends with the shadows.

In a wooden chair near the window, moonlight spotlights an incubus sitting up straight with posture so perfect it's easy to note his royal lineage. His black irises focus solely on the glittering dust swirling in his hands.

I don't know why I expect to see a pretty picture of me.

Or even a dirty drawing of my orgasm.

But that's not what he envisions for us all to see. A tall man with twisting horns juts out from Krave's fingertips. His hooves are nothing more than a pile of glitter glued to the demon's hand. And it seems very much so that no matter how hard he frantically turns and tries to move, he's nailed in place.

Until Krave's long black fingers arch, and he closes his palm so hard the magic sprays out from between his hard-lined knuckles.

I blink at the thought of how easily Krave could have killed the councilman.

He could have, but he was right. That sort of revenge would solve nothing. He would simply come right back.

That logic is no longer there, though. Dark shadows

77

circle Krave's eyes as he looks up at me with more self-hate than I've ever seen in him in all the time I've known him.

"Krave." I cross the room slowly and it's then that I note the mound of a man sleeping on the bed in the shadowy corner. Ryke rests while Krave seems to reminisce about every failure he's ever created in his long, endless life.

And I just know he critically counts them all, one by one by one.

This is how he was after I'd found out he was a spy for my father. He was a shell of self loathing. But he'd pulled out of it. Because he loved me more than he loved himself. I think *I* love him more than he loves himself too. And I won't leave him here in the darkness of his mind.

He doesn't look up at me and the pressure in my chest presses harder until I lower myself, my hands sliding over his thighs while I hunch down between his black shoes. "Krave," I whisper once more.

The blackness of his gaze is a bleeding look that spiderwebs out past his slashing brows and down the sharp lines of his cheek bones. His attention spans slowly to me. My heart cracks against my ribs as I wait for an inkling of an emotion to cross his sullen features.

Nothing shows there, though. A vast emptiness is set in there, and the only notion that he sees me at all is when he lifts his cold hand and slides his fingers ever so lightly down my jaw. He caresses me like the petals of a flower. He'll never let me bruise.

But how hurt is he on the inside? How many bruises does he hide?

"Come here Krave," I say quietly, but sternly.

His head tilts at me and I know it's confusing. I know

he's barely processing any of this. So instead, I pull his thighs hard and bring him down to me. He stumbles down to my level and once he goes down to his knees, he keeps on going. He lowers like he might just lie down and die here in this cottage of a home.

But I won't let him.

My arms wrap around his lean frame until his temple meets my shoulder, giving me his weight while I just cling to him like it's the last thing I'll ever do in my life.

For tonight, it will be.

Because saving Krave from himself is far more important than any vengeance I may seek.

And I have *a lot* of vengeance to attend to.

CHAPTER ELEVEN
A GLAMOUR

Aries

The sun shines blinding light into the room that faces East, catching the brunt of the heat provided by the morning daylight. Ryke got up hours ago. Damien now rests in his spot on the bed that must have originally been Krave's.

It should be odd how close these men seem now. They were strangers, once upon a time. Love does that though. And losing love like they lost me and Zaviar, that would unite even the deadliest of enemies to ever walk Hell and Earth.

"Is he going to be okay?" Damien asks quietly.

He sits with his back to the headboard as he watches

me curl up on the floor with my sweet, sleeping incubus.

Is he going to be okay?

"I don't know." My fingers stroke through soft black hair. "Maybe… Yes. Yes he'll be okay." I nod with more certainty.

"How do you know?"

I arch a brow at that, and shift against the soreness of my muscles. Sleeping on the floor has brought me new pains.

"I know because Krave and I are similar in that way. Our hate drives us sometimes. And our revenge… that's on a different level of motivation entirely.

I feel Damien studying me. His attention is a careful scrutiny.

"You have a Queen of Hell in your soul, Aries," his tone is steady but quiet. "That Seraph king, or whatever he is, can't touch you."

I pause to wait for Catherine to chime in.

But she must be as tired as I am. Silence is the only reply.

"He can't fuck with any of us. You have enough problems. Maybe you should let this g—"

"What about Zaviar?" I ask harshly without giving him the time to finish. "Zaviar isn't a fallen. He isn't like you. He isn't like *us!*" My tone rises so much that a gentle hand slides down to my wrist and my gaze flits down to find beautiful demonic eyes looking up at me.

"You're salacious when you yell at other men, darling." Krave's voice is scratchy but warm.

And most importantly, the lines around his eyes have vanished as he looks up at me.

SPITEFUL CREATURES

"But do try to cut him some slack. He isn't the brightest of your harem," Krave explains as he stands without a single stretch or any sign of discomfort from sleeping on a fucking hardwood floor all night.

He takes my hand and brings me up against his tall frame, as if last night never happened. He even smiles down on me with a beaming gleam of his white teeth. He's so handsome.

More importantly, he's so resilient. My heart flutters to life just seeing how the sunlight washes into him like it's drawn to him as much as I am.

"Did you just call me stupid?" Damien growls, and our sweet moment tumbles away as a white pillow collides into Krave's perfect black hair. The pillow falls to the ground with a sad flump. Krave's hair is flattened on one side and standing tall on the other.

The Prince of Hell cuts his friend a slicing glare as he smooths down the messy locks on his head. "A real man uses his words first, and his fists directly after. But never a pillow." Krave's smirk appears rather manically and he offers Damien a wink at the end that just leaves the man more confused.

"Glad to see you're back to normal," Ryke says from the hall, leaning into the white frame of the door, his big black wings taking up the entire space there.

"Now, as for problem solving," Krave addresses the room. "I have a feeling you're right, Aries. They'll come looking for Zaviar."

"Why haven't they just beamed him up?" I ask and even Damien and Ryke clearly want to know that answer.

"Because of you." Krave taps the tip of my nose with his finger, but I shake the gesture off as he continues on.

"You're anchoring him to yourself with your bond. Realms should never separate mates. The magic that splits the realms apart, it's nothing compared to magic of the heart."

He sounds so sentimental that my actual heart beats faster because of his sweet little words.

"What about when Zaviar and Aries went to the Bliss? That separated us from her." Damien's sitting up even more now, his hands resting on his knees as he listens intently.

"That's because…" Krave waves his hands this way and that, as if he doesn't want to say it, but we all know he eventually will.

… Maybe.

"It's because I died." I blink through my blunt statement. I guess I hadn't really come to terms with that. The dead silence that drops into the room tells me that the other three men hadn't either.

"Going to the Bliss saved her. It may have even changed her some, but the bond we share is still strong."

"How do I get my bond to totally disconnect theirs?" I ask him.

Krave lifts his fingers with a dwindling sort of thought. "Have you ever considered having him snort some royal demonic ashes? I hear possession can be quite durable." The seriousness of his face makes me want to slap him harder.

Possession. Because that worked so great on me.

Once more I wait.

Catherine says nothing.

I don't know why her silence lingers like anxiety crushing my lungs. She'd been quieter and quieter, but never silent.

SPITEFUL CREATURES

I shake the thought away. There's too much on my plate right now for me to worry over the little old poltergeist not having an opinion for once.

"I'm going to the Kingdom of Roses' castle. My sister's book of spells will have something."

"Are you going to kill her while you stop in for a visit?" Krave suggests.

The room pauses on that question like it's serious.

"Not today." I stride to the door and Ryke steps aside for me to pass, my soft feathers brushing against his smooth wing.

"Why… doesn't he just start the process of falling?" Ryke asks quietly as he follows closely behind me.

"Why didn't you?" I turn on him when we get to the small dining room. A table sits in the far left corner while a little sink and oven line the opposite wall. My mother quietly watches from near the oven as she sips from a small cup, the scent of lavender tea fills the air, and it calms me just slightly.

"Because… I'm an angel."

And there you have it. He's a hundred years old, delayed the demonic process in a painful, twisting way, and yet he still considers himself an angel.

"And Zaviar tried his damnedest to keep Damien an angel as well. None of you are property of the Torch. But none of you will ever feel like you belong in any realm other than the Bliss."

"I—" he pauses, and the gentle way he takes my hand eases all the frustration right out of me, "I belong with you. In whatever realm, Aries. I belong with you."

My soul shivers and I close my eyes slowly as I just fall

into that sensation for a little while.

"Zaviar will feel the same way," he whispers.

Maybe… but I can't imagine my pink feathered Seraph as anything other than what he is.

"I just want to see what our options are. I'll check the spells, and we can decide from there." I pull the front door open, my hand sliding from his but before I take one step out of the house she speaks.

"Take your lovers, dear!" My mother calls after me.

And I shrink back just from that one word alone.

Lovers.

"They're my mates, Mom!" My tight-lipped smile must be something you inherently learn from being a child.

I still have it in me though. And I give her that awkward smile now.

"Right. Take your boyfriends with you though. It's not safe there any more." She looks at me with her big green eyes.

"I don't need their help. Besides, it's never really been safe there," I whisper back to her.

And I don't linger on the sadness in her gaze as I stride out.

I hate the bitter honesty of my words, but I hate that she acts as if that truth doesn't exist even more.

Three men follow quietly behind me as I leave the safety of that little cottage in the woods. The feel of its quiet isolation slips away with every step I take.

Because the panicked pounding of my heart is a warning of what's to come.

* * *

SPITEFUL CREATURES

The shadows have always been my friend. As my back melds against the cold walls of the castle, the darkness of the night curling sweetly around me, I'm reminded of our relationship once more.

And as Ryke thunders into Damien's side for the second time, I'm also reminded that these men and I do not have an open relationship with my first lover, the darkness.

"Would you pick up the fucking pace?" Ryke growls.

Damien turns on him, and it's Krave turn to be the peacemaker.

Kind of.

"Listen, listen: I'll gladly thrust in between you two if we're going to be pounding into one another all night." He waves his hand like it'll be a real inconvenience, but he's willing to take one for the team.

Okay, he's not really a peacemaker. But he does shut them both up as they're scowling at him now, instead of each other.

"I'm going in. You're all waiting outside."

"I feel like I've heard that line before," Ryke says, folding his arms solidly over his chest.

…Right…

"I can go in." Krave steps forward. "I can go unnoticed. You two can't sneak down a hall for more than two seconds without your cocks slapping against one another."

Okay he is definitely not the peacemaker.

"*Fuck you!*" Ryke hisses.

Dammit, why did mother insist they come? I told her I didn't need help.

No one ever listens to me.

And now look at where it's gotten me: into a pissing contest outside the castle of doom.

"Can you three hold it the fuck together for one minute?" At the sound of my harsh scream of a whisper, silence finally settles between them.

Fucking finally.

"I'm going to take you somewhere, and none of you are ever to speak of it again," I instruct with all seriousness.

"I love this already," Krave says as the other two nod.

I shake my head, but quietly lead them to the far side of the castle. The aroma of roses faintly wafts through the chilled night air, but my mother's beautiful garden is just out of sight. Instead, I stop at an old brick that sticks out just slightly uneven from the others along the western wall.

The Shadow Guard would kill me right now if they knew.

"Well well well. If it isn't the twice removed Princess of Roses." The cruel cutting tone isn't hushed at all. It's spoken freely and emerges like the first rays of an eclipse from the darkness.

My eyes close slowly, simply to stop myself from glaring at him.

"Sev," I say somewhat politely through clenched teeth.

I turn to my fellow Shadow Guard. The smirk I expect to find on his face isn't there. Dark scruff highlights his olive skin.

"We need your help," he tells me without any further bullshit as he pushes open the invisible door, swinging the brick wall fully open to the back of the Shadow Guards hidden room. The light is scarce once inside. Filing cabinets block our view, so the four of us have to zig-zag our way through the small room and into the area where the real work takes place.

But the tables, and the mess of paperwork… it's all abandoned.

No one else is here.

"Where is everyone?" I ask, peering over my shoulder the three men behind me as they take it all in.

"We've scattered. The Pixies are small. They can follow without being seen. Better than us, even. It's too risky for a spy to be planted with thousands of other spies playing for the enemy. Some of us have been searching for you. Others were sent away." Sev plops down into a wooden chair and the simple way his shoulder sag tells me it's been harder than he's letting on. "Your sister isn't interrogating people like your father once did. She doesn't care about money or even punishment like he did. If she suspects someone as an informant, or a traitor, she just kills them." His dark eyes lift and settle on mine in a hopeless gaze.

"I'll fix it," I whisper, my chin tipping up despite how uncertain I really am.

He studies me a moment longer.

"Good," he finally says. "Keep your fucking friends here. Do what you have to do. But the Pixies, they'll find you. And you'll need someone to tell your mother when they do."

An unexpected shiver crawls through me.

"They won't." Once more I force a certainty I don't feel into those words.

He shrugs. "Good."

I make my way towards the door, but I only take a single step before a warm hand wraps around mine. I'm pulled back and a hard chest slams into me, taking me against him and scattering my determination all to hell.

Then soft lips skim along mine. And Damien kisses me like he'll never see me again.

"I'll see you soon," he whispers with more confidence than either of us feel.

My heartbeat doubles as he kisses me tenderly once more.

And I suddenly feel the assurance.

Maybe it's mine and maybe it's his, but I have it now.

I nod to him, looking at my three men as I slowly back away from them, memorizing the watchful shine of their eyes. My hand wraps around the cool knob of the door and I open it even as I look back at them. I feel their gazes as I finally turn away.

"Fucking Romeo," I hear Ryke curse.

That's the last thing I hear from them as I pull the door closed, locking them inside. Out of sight and safely away from the dangers of this court.

I stand in the unlit span of the kitchens. The moonlight glitters over a few pots and utensils left out by the cooks.

I should be more prepared, but at the last minute I send a flare of my magic all through my body, morphing my image into what I need others to see me as. My limbs shrink. My long silver hair turns to strands of gleaming gold while my stark black wings turn illuminescent. The tiny things flutter like gold dust in the meager lighting. And when I curse a good "fuck," it comes out as an angry little squeak.

Ah, the way of the Pixies.

Even their anger sounds cute.

We have so much in common.

Everything around me is enormous and it honestly takes me just too damn long to figure out which way I'm flying.

"Fucking gnats with egos the size of dragon cocks, I tell you." Which translates to: "Squeak, with squeak squeak, squeak. Squeak the squeak cocks, squeak."

I'm already speaking their lingo.

My wings beat hard, almost as fast as my racing heart, and I'm stunned by how fast I move. Everything's a blur around me.

So much so, that a thump sounds at the same time as my entire body aches, mainly my face. Wind slips through my hair and glittering wings and another dose of pain is ordered up as I hit the ground, hard.

"*Fuck!*" I hiss on a squeak.

"Fuck is right," someone agrees with a booming, terrifying voice.

I blink, and it takes my eyes several seconds to trail up the goblin's once small frame.

Nille.

He shifts from one little leg to the other.

"You shouldn't be here," he whispers, but it sounds loud and ominous to me.

His big head turns from side to side as he looks both ways down the dark corridor. His wide eyes eat up everything, including my fake glamour. "You mother barely got out with her life. Why are you back now?"

A better question would be why is he still here?

"You're spying for my mother," I accuse in my absurdly mousey voice.

"Hush," he points a thick finger my way. "And get on with whatever you're here to do. Murder, I suspect."

I shake my head adamantly. An exaggerated *I'd never!* sort of shake.

But we both know that I would.

Just… not at the moment.

My wings flutter daintily—far more sweetly than my real wings could have in my entire life—and meet him at eye level… well, his big ass goblin eye to my entire pixie body, that is.

And we stare at one another. Understanding one another in a single moment.

"She rushed to the tower." He looks both ways once more, and he doesn't say another word as he makes his way downstairs as if he never crossed paths with an exiled, dead princess who shouldn't be here.

And I fly up like pixie dust in the wind. So fucking fast that I'm stunned I don't kill myself crashing into a high hanging chandelier. The circular twirling round and round of the tower staircase has my little brain spinning, and I make the choice to dissolve my glamour. I use my magic to flutter those pretty glittering wings back into enormous raven black feathers. Wafting silver hairs fan out around my waist as I seep into the shadows, hiding myself away as I get closer and closer to the top. My breath stills in my lungs as moonlight floods toward me. I hug the cold wall. Wind swirls in and I hear her voice first.

"I told you to stop coming here!" Corva growls so lowly that I swear the demonic side of her is physically crawling out.

When I peer out though, her transparent black hair is the same as I remember. The dress that washes around her is a shadow of a gown, and everything about her screams death and decay.

But the white-horned man towering over her doesn't flinch.

"And I said you had by the end of the week to deliver him. I know you have my Seraph. He's bound to your bloodline." Darine has the audacity to pick up a lock of my sister's long black hair, it drifts right through his hand, but I just know he's inches from death.

If he could be, that is.

"Do not touch me," she hisses.

He tips his head down, his smooth cheek coming oh so close to hers. "If you do not get me Zaviar, I will do far worse than that, My Pretty Queen," he whispers sickly.

Shit.

I slink into the darkness and I don't wait to listen to the two of them argue or hate fuck or whatever it is their screwed up relationship is.

Because I need that book! Now more than ever.

My steps are like wind against the pavement as I run down the stairs. I'm full on sprinting to the room just outside the tower. It's a cold and drafty compartment that no one has used in years.

Because it was hers.

And I just know she'd feel safest here.

When I fling the door open and shut it quickly behind myself, I find that I was right. Stacks of black leather-bound books sit on an entry table to my right. Long dark cloaks hang on a rack to my left.

And yet, I know she wouldn't keep something so personal right out in the open.

It feels… terrifying to walk further into her bedroom. It's a small space, no larger than the rooms back at the cottage. But, as a little girl, I learned early not to touch my sister's things. She was sweet on me back then, but she was still a big sister.

And she was protective of her things. The few things she owned, that is.

So the sensation that I might be caught and under her wrath for being here is a fond childhood memory. Except now I won't be facing mommy and daddy for my wrong doings.

I'll be facing death.

With trepidation I walk toward the twin bed in the center of the room. My hand slips under the mattress and my arm extends to the fullest as I sweep over the tight space there. I do it on one side and then the other.

A coldness and a bit of dust can be felt along my fingertips.

But there's nothing else to be found there.

My gaze scans the space. I distractedly lift the pillows. I open the drawers to her nightstand and dresser, but I know she's far cleverer than that.

"Where is it?" I whisper to myself.

Her wardrobe is an old rickety wooden box with a broken lock on the front. It was grandmother Hyval's when she was a girl. It was grandmother's, and Corva loved it dearly.

I take a few steps toward it. My fingers wrap around

the cool metal and it shifts loosely in my palm when I pull.

Dust scurries out. But in the dimness of the light...

I see it.

The gleaming crown sits high on the top shelf, and I know for a fact a speck of our brother's blood still adorns the deep encrusted jewels. My hand drops away from it in an instant.

But beneath the crown that I killed my brother with, sits a book.

A tattered paged journal.

The spell book.

It's worn and used. The spine is cracked from top to bottom, and the dark covering has a soft discoloration from decades of being picked up, carried, and flat out loved.

If I take it, she'll kill me.

Again.

With a lift of my hand and a brush of smooth, worn leather, the spine is caressed like an old friend. My fingers arch and with only my index and thumb, I pick up the heavy crown like the cursed heirloom that it is. I set it down without a sound just to the right of the book.

The tassels of the hangman's knot at the front of the cover tease my fingertips...

And then... and then it's mine.

I'm suddenly aware of how quiet the room is as I gaze down on the one thing that I know will save Zaviar from his own makers. It has the power to prevent demons from becoming demons. I know it'll have the answers to stop an angel from being an angel.

It's strange how mundane it seems at this moment.

"It's just a book," I whisper to myself.

"Yeah, and we need to go." A breathless voice urges from behind me. A shiver startles down my spine from the simple sound of someone else so close to me.

I spin on my heels, dropping the textbook to the floor with a toppling thump. Ryke stands in the hall, gripping the door frame so hard I hear the faint crack of splinters as he stares at me with wide eyes.

"A little goblin man said a high born Seraph and a fucking demon queen bitch are storming the castle. Looking for Zaviar. *And you!*" He checks the hall, looking one way and then the other. "Lets go. Now!"

The chaotic symphony of my heart plays on repeat in my ears until the rush of it kicks my ass into gear. I scoop up the book, slip it into the back of my jeans and let the weight of my wings settle against the stolen object like it never existed in the first place.

And then I fucking run.

The bedroom, the halls, the stairwell, no windows bless us as we soar down to the first floor on open wings and speeding steps. The kitchen is silent in the dark, and the seamless door to the Shadow Guard's office is just as close as the big windows.

"Damien and Krave are only waiting outside for three minutes. Let's go!" Ryke motions to the door for me to open it.

But I've stopped in my tracks. The heartbeat that was drumming through me just moments ago has halted abruptly. As has my breathing.

Because standing like a bad omen in the corner of the dark room, is a seven foot tall angelic monster.

SPITEFUL CREATURES

"It's nice to see you again, Aries," he hums like white noise.

The clack of his hooves against the flooring is as unsettling as his pale but ominous features. Shadows cut across the hard lines of his cheekbones and that darkness seems to cling to the spiral of his horns and wings.

He looks like Hell Lord got a makeover.

Ryke shifts, one foot taking a single step in front of mine, but I know he'd never make me feel so weak as to come between me and a new life-long enemy. Instead, he watches the eerie man with every muscle in his body tensed to its full massive size.

"You as well." I plant my hands firmly on my hips as I address the scariest mother fucker I've ever encountered in my life. "Glad to see my incubus didn't completely cripple you."

My taunting words visibly hit a nerve as his left eye twitches, but he never loses that crooked sneer against his lips.

"Where is my Seraph?" he growls so deeply the tone of his question scurries through the hanging pots and pans.

"I'm sorry, I don't know who you mean. Can you be more specific?"

And then he lunges.

The span of white feathers is his giveaway.

He's quick and he's evil, but he hasn't lived his life fighting assholes just like himself as I have. I'm fucking ready.

My hand lurches out. Ryke steps aside, spinning on his boots to give me room. It's a blur of movements. A choreographed dance of adrenaline.

But I've never been so focused on revenge before.

My nails sink into his flesh in midair. He and I levitate

with the soft beats of our wings, then with a shove of my arm I bring him down to the darkness of the kitchen floor by the spindly muscles of his throat. I sink my fingers in harder and he gasps as he hits the ground with breathless impact.

"You're not in the Bliss anymore, mother fucker!" I push against the firmness of his windpipe as I straddle over his skinny chest and really grip with both hands. "Do not come into my fucking kingdom and make demands!" His hands grapple at my arms and it feels good to feel him struggle.

The way I know he made Zaviar struggle.

"I've been told, when I kill you, you'll simply reincarnate into your vile ass right back in the Bliss again." I tighten my hold so hard he chokes on a lack of air. "I guess we'll find out."

The whites of his eyes are a telling sign as they roll back into his skull. My weight bares down harder. His nails no longer scratch at the flesh of my arms. My muscles tighten even more as I lift up, arching my back to fully press everything I have into ending his disgusting life.

It's there.

I can feel the unsteady beat of his heart against my palms. I see the struggle leave him.

The clatter of metal slamming to the floor jars my attention and a gasp of air and rejuvenation sounds beneath me as I turn toward the counter in the middle of the room and find Ryke pinned there with his limbs reaching to all four corners. The leathery wings at his back tremble. He grunts. He thrashes.

But he's held there by an unseen hand.

"Tsk, tsk, tsk," she says.

SPITEFUL CREATURES

Something black flings toward me, and it catches hard against the side of my head with a ringing slap against my skull. The pan clatters to the floor just as I do.

Councilman Darine crawls away from me, abandoning his kitchen ready weapon as he grovels over to the feet of my sister.

"Aries," she hisses as she slithers closer. The whisking of her form, the apparition of her wings and the darkness of her clothes are all a ghostly appearance. "I missed you," she purrs.

The hard outline of the book pressing into my back is suddenly painfully apparent. I'm very aware of the one thing that will sign my own death warrant in the blink of an eye.

"We should have stuck together," I tell her, my gaze still blurred and my head still ringing with pain. "We're alike. We're too alike, and you know it. No one's ever been outsiders in this kingdom like the two royal-born sisters of King Gravier." My chin lifts, but I can't focus on the skeptical look in her eyes. "We should stick together."

My magic isn't deadly like hers. I'm made to deceive. While she's made to destroy.

But when she lowers her hand and I hear Ryke take a solid inhale of air for the first time in several minutes, I truly know the bond of blood that we share is enough to save our lives.

Then her hand rises once more, but instead of attacking me with her long polished nails, she spins that power directly on me. It isn't a crushing sensation that cripples me to the ground, it's a feeling of smoke burning my lungs. My back arches against the cold floor while I grasp against the air itself as I choke for a breath.

With tears streaming down my cheeks, her face appears just above me. The long black hair of hers clings to her sharp features.

"We were once sisters, Aries. I'll never forget those kindred years. But I'll also never forget the time I spent isolated, alone and talking to only the sound of my own voice. I used that time to realize, I can only trust myself. So I don't trust you enough to ever bind myself with you the way you were stupid enough to. I know that, in time, you'll kill me. And that means, dear sister, that I must kill you first."

There isn't any joy in her features as the room shadows her gaze that's looming down on me. Her brow bends, and I can tell she doesn't want to end the only person who's ever loved her in her long life.

But a determined woman is the most terrifying thing in the world.

As well as the most underestimated.

Black spots flash around the edges of my sight and my erratic heart finally calms a little as I stare up at the woman who used to be my only friend as a child. The memory warms me in a funny way. Peace settles into me as the distant sound of laughter in a maze of roses dances in the darkness at the back of my mind.

I stop struggling. My hands go limp at my sides.

I knew she'd kill me. I knew because she and I are the same in that way. Protect yourself above all else. Because you're disposable. Emotions are a weakness. They'll get you killed.

Just like my emotions for Zaviar have gotten me killed now.

Just as my eyes close, I think I hear someone familiar

finally speak within my thoughts. It's a whisper like the wind, and I can even feel it.

And then her face flashes through my mind: Black, sharp arched brows frame dark and powerful hazel eyes. She doesn't smile at me, and although I've only ever seen her ashes, I recognize her pale face in an instant.

Catherine.

Her image flickers once more before fading into the calm that is my peaceful mind.

I'm going to fix this for you, stupid girl.

What?

I said I'm going to do something. And it better not be for nothing, so pay attention! I've been melding into you for years. I've fought it in hopes of returning to the Torch. But you're my resting place now. Your heartbeat has been my own. And the fire inside you, it's the same as mine was.

Her strong features flash once more, but with a pained look in her eyes as she stares right into me.

You saved me once. Long after I'd died and everyone had forgotten about the hellacious Queen buried in the wrong realm out of petty jealousy. But you saved me from your father just to protect demons who wouldn't have done the same for a stupid royal born girl. So, pay attention. And I'll thank you for the struggles you've sacrificed. Pay attention, Aries.

Pay attention.

Pay…

The sound of glass shatters through my drifting thoughts of the beautiful but haunting Queen who loved a man who was never meant to be hers. Something fiery hot burns through my body. My blood. My bones.

The image of her is no longer in my mind. Her voice is a faded echo. But the power of her existence scorches through me so deep I scream out in trembling agony.

And then I sleep.

CHAPTER TWELVE
RECKLESS BEAUTY
Ryke

She weighs nothing. Damn wings weigh as much as she does. How can the smallest woman I've ever met be so gods damn reckless?

Her head nuzzles into my shoulder with a breathy sound, and the irritation of her almost dying sizzles right out of me. Her shining black horns are cold against my flesh. My arms curl around her harder and I want to just hold her for the rest of our fucking lives to ensure she never throws herself in harms away again.

But I know she will.

Again and again and again.

Krave walks ahead through the forest without saying a word. *For once.*

He's a strange creature. On the day to day, he looks like he'd pull balloon animals right out of his ass while giggling sky-high on helium.

But then when she's in trouble, like she was tonight, he's monstrous. He looks like he could burn this entire fucking realm to the ground to save her.

And I fully believe he would.

We all would.

My attention flicks to the other psycho who loves her. Damien's still clutching his bloody arm that's wrapped up in his shirt. The idiot used it to break his fall as he broke through the biggest window in the whole damn castle. While Krave just fluttered in after him like a butterfly discovering a particularly pretty flower.

Until he saw Aries lying lifelessly on the floor that is.

He'd locked eyes with that bitch and it was that distraction that gave me time to hurtle her to the fucking ground. Damien joined me, but Krave went right for Aries. He had her for a moment, too.

Until that white hooved motherfucker donkey kicked his ass.

I don't know what the fuck he was, but I know Corva alone is too powerful for the three of us. We've seen her magic in the past. And the goal was to get Aries out alive.

Even if Damien had to drag Krave away from the white winged demon he kept lashing back out at.

"He almost got her killed," Damien hisses, eyes held firmly on the slender man ahead of us.

SPITEFUL CREATURES

The two men have a love hate relationship between them. But it seems Aries' safety comes first.

As it should.

I think back to how vengeful the incubus looked. Hellfire burned in the black depths of his eyes and he kept going after him even after Corva had turned the room on its axis, swirling with debris and power.

Did he know that white winged devil?

"It was the councilman," she whispers along my neck,

A shiver races over my flesh from the warmth of her breath and all three of us stop walking to look down at her. Long black lashes fan with slow blinks of her gorgeous eyes.

"Krave…"

"I'm here." He's hovering, his head nearly touching mine as he presses himself against my arms to be near her.

"We can't kill them," she says with a bitter smile. She closes her eyes once more as her head settles heavily against my shoulder again.

I look around at the two other men before hurriedly ushering her the last few yards to the cottage up ahead. My boot meets the door and I'm storming into the house like a vicious warrior, simply to set her down in the warm comfort of a bed.

I lie her down with so much gentle care, just for her to roll off of me and sit up facing the three men taking up all the space in this tiny room.

"Lie down," I nearly growl at her.

She's so fucking reckless. Even with herself.

"We can't kill them."

"You said that already. Now lie down. You need your

rest." I make a move towards her like I'll wrestle her to the fucking pillow if I have to.

"Cathrine can," she blurts, as if all my menacing means nothing.

"What? Lie down." At that I do lunge for her, but she side rolls off the bed and with a flip of her hair and ruffle of her wings, she lands on her feet at the end of the mattress. And a little brown book is in her hand.

"Cathrine," Krave repeats.

"Get your ass in bed!" I fully yell at her this time.

And among my annoyance and everyone else's lunacy, Damien says one thing that finally makes some sort of fucking sense.

"That's Corva's spell book." He looks wide eyed at the thing that prevented his twisted, demonic transformation.

As well as my own.

Shit.

She actually got it.

CHAPTER THIRTEEN

A NIGHT OF HEAVEN AND HELL

Aries

I should feel beaten. Broken. Definitely bruised.

But I don't.

I feel healthier than I have in my entire life. The muscle tone seems fuller around my petite biceps. The magic in my veins is a roaring sound like the ocean filling my ears. Even the shine of my silver hair is more luxurious.

But my heart feels empty.

Because I always had this idea in my head that I'd somehow vomit Cathrine back up—gracefully of course—and lay her to rest in the realm of Hell.

I can never do that now. She sacrificed herself somehow. She… gave what remained of herself to save me.

And that's a gift of life that I can never repay.

I can only make sure it's used in a way that will help others.

Starting with Zaviar.

I have to dodge and then duck past Ryke's enormous frame to run out into the hall. And when I enter Zav's room, he's buttoning a pair of black jeans around his slim, but scarred hips.

Nasty red lines scratch up his knuckles, his forearms, his biceps and chest. Even his handsome face.

My heart sinks when I meet his pretty iron-like eyes. It's my fault.

Everything that's bad in their lives is my fucking fault.

"Stop," Zaviar whispers.

"I'm so fucking sorry," I confess on a breathless tone that barely passes my lips.

Dampness stings my eyes because it's harder now that he's up. He's alive. He's awake and standing. But he'll never be the same.

"Stop," he says softly once more, taking my hands in his, letting the worn book slip out of my fingers and down to the floor. His warm palm slides up my arm and slowly across my neck before tipping my chin up to give himself my full attention. "Get that guilty look out of your eyes."

I blink hard, but it just causes more tears to fall.

"If it weren't for you, Damien would be a demon. Ryke would be your sister's lacky. Krave would be a fuckboy prince in the Torch—"

"That's true," Krave pipes up.

SPITEFUL CREATURES

A smile reaches my eyes, but just barely.

"And I would be living the rest of my long and miserable life in the Bliss. Without my brother... and without the one woman I love more than anything in all the realms."

My heartbeat flutters, dips, and soars all at once.

He whispered it once before. It was his confessed secret to keep.

And now it's real.

"I love you too," I say so breathlessly it hurts. It hurts to know he loves me after everything I've put him through.

"I was bound to get scars along the way as a piece of property to the Bliss. At least this way, they will be worth something." His fingers are gentle along my jaw and he skims them even higher as he tangles them through my hair and pulls me into him, hard.

And then his lips seal against mine.

There are so many things I want to say. I want apologies to spill out like a flood, but the swirl of his tongue against mine washes all those words away. He devours my shame and guilt. He kisses me like he's healing the both of us with just the sinuous way his mouth moves over mine.

His hand in my hair twists just slightly, causing a moan of pain and pleasure to hum through me. While someone else awakens more of me. Their warm and tempting hand skims its way along my spine. It's a soft touch, gentle and exploring. I faintly become aware that two more hands have joined in.

I pull back from Zaviar just long enough to feel the blazing gaze of Damien's attention as he slips his fingers down and begins unbuttoning my jeans. A gasp barely has time to leave my lips before I'm pulled toward someone else whose bright green eyes look deviously into mine as Ryke kisses me slowly.

Hands caresses me from all angles. Krave's whispered words of appreciation flit through the room and I feel them along my spine as he kisses lower and lower and lower. And then my jeans are tugged down. And Krave's mouth keeps going down, down, down.

I struggle to think as lips and hands and delicious ecstasy consumes me. It isn't like last time. This time, it feels softer. Slower. Painfully slower.

"Please," I beg as a hand ghosts over the lace of my panties.

But it never pushes hard enough to fill the ache that's spreading there.

Warm breath fans along the curve of my ass, and it's just a hint of sensation that keeps flitting away as the admirer skims his slender fingers up and down my thighs.

"Fuck, please!" I tremble hard when Zaviar's teeth scrape down the curve of my neck and Ryke kisses me harder, sucking on my tongue until I'm a puddle in all their hands.

I'm theirs to use however they want. As long as they satisfy the pulsing demand that's surging within me.

More light and torturous kisses press along my legs and then, slowly, slide between my thighs. But they stop abruptly over the thin material covering my most intimate skin.

When I shake hard, I nearly stumble. A rumbling laugh fans along my flesh there.

SPITEFUL CREATURES

The asshole.

Hot warmth presses over the lace, and with a heavy press of their tongue they sweep over me from entrance to clit so hard that I become desperate.

My hand snatches Ryke's jaw and I kiss him so deeply it hurts with bruising strength against my lips. But he simply growls low, with a hint of warning in his tone before his big hands grip my hips and he throws me. My wings splay out in mid air and I land on the bed with a soft and delicate display of poise.

My wings are so sore. But at this moment, I don't feel it.

All four men look at me with wide-eyed interest. I sit with my wings arched out and lift my hand to admire my nails, like I'm not completely breathless and needy. Instead, I channel the inner goddess that they always make me feel like.

And I take control of the outnumbered situation.

"The first to make me cum gets to fuck me," I tell them with a confident tilt of my chin.

Ryke and Zaviar pass each other a judging gaze, sizing one another up like they can see the other's orgasm inducing skills just with a quick glance. Damien looks to Krave and Krave simply smiles, like two are better than one.

Then the incubus lifts his long fingers and caresses Damien's hard jawline.

"Come here," he tells his friend intimately. There is such a longing glint in their eyes before Krave brings his attention back down to me.

And I can't help the way my thighs shift together as

the two of them crawl up the blankets. With a push of each of their hands, they spread me open for them. They position themselves comfortably between my calves, Damien resting on his knees while Krave lies on his stomach like he's picking daisies in a field of heavenly relaxation. Swift fingers skim up the long expanse of my legs before coming higher and higher to the softest part of my thighs, sweeping over my flesh like a breath of steamy air. Krave brushes over the apex of my hip before diverting down to feel the heat at my center. But he doesn't stay there, he trails up and curls his fingers around the waist of my panties and slowly pulls them down my legs.

As the feel of the rough fabric travels down my thighs and legs, the mattress dips on either side. Ryke wraps his fingers all the way around my wrist and I raise my hand as if to reach for his head and bring him nearer.

Except he slams my hand down high above my head. The restraint of it shoves a gasp from my lungs. He smiles slow and deliciously while his other palm travels roughly against my stomach, pushing at my shirt as he travels over my ribs and the soft mounds of my breast before brushing ever so lightly over my nipple.

And then I'm shaking. My legs tremble, but two firm hands press down against my thighs. Another takes my free hand, but instead of pinning it down, he drags it across his hard muscle tone.

I look up at Zaviar as he guides my fingers over the lines of scars along his abdomen. But I'm not even aware of the wounds now. I'm entirely focused on how his nerves jump with each brush of my hand against his powerful body. Especially as he slides his jeans down lower, and runs my own hand down the length of his shaft.

SPITEFUL CREATURES

"The goal is to make her cum, not the other way around," Krave murmurs as he flicks his tongue teasingly above where I want him most.

Zav gives a half-smirk at his words. "You know, some people get off on pleasing others," Zaviar's hooded eyes hold mine.

"I'm very aware," Krave hums. And then his mouth fully devours my sex.

I gasp, my fingers tightening around the thick, rigidness of Zaviar's pulsing cock.

"That's a good girl," Zaviar tells me, his hips flexing just slightly as my hand slides up and then slowly back down.

The roll of Krave's tongue shifts and then a second mouth seals itself right next to his. Then I close my eyes as a moan consumes me entirely. Their tongues brush along my most sensitive spot, twirling together, and swirling and sucking and just making me insane with the thought of the two of them wanting me so much they have to share.

My hand that's held firmly into the pillow lunges to thrust into Damien's soft hair, but the hold on my wrist only tightens. Infuriatingly so.

"*Fuck,*" I hiss out, but the word is stifled as another mouth presses to mine.

His beard is rough against my skin, but his teeth sinking into my lower lips is even more pained erotica. A whimper slips out, but Ryke kisses the sound away with a gentler touch. His nails release from how deeply they were pressed into my flesh as he lets go of my hand. He pulls back entirely. When his sweet eyes meet mine, I let my hand slide away from Zaviar to give my fallen angel all of my attention.

"Take your pants off," I command with a gasp of reckless pleasure.

His eyebrows lift, but he does as he's told rather quickly before coming right back to my side. He leans into my hand but I push off from the bed and my tongue glides down his shaft before he can even realize what I'm doing.

"Shhhhhhit!" His hand thrusts through my hair and he takes his time gathering the long silver locks away from my face. More for his own benefit than mine.

His rhythm takes only a second to match the slide of my lips as I take every single inch of him as deep as I can. He hits the back of my throat against and again, and I love the way his curses and groans mingle together as I take him a little deeper.

Two fingers tease my slit, up and down and up and down, before sinking in deep. My sounds of pleasure are a weak noise that's consumed with how much deeper Ryke fucks my throat. I'm a mess of limbs. My arms are holding me up to give Ryke my attention while my ass is held firmly in what I can only assume are Damien's kneading hands. The pressure of tongues and the curve of fingers tightens the feelings furling deep inside my core until I'm a panting wreck around a demanding hardness that fills my mouth completely.

I moan and scream, but the men don't stop their thrusting, their sucking, or their grinding against me. Krave's palm against my sex barely moves as his fingers pound harder and harder at just the right spot deep inside, and the mouth fully around my clit slides their tongue all the way up and as far down as it can go before sucking hard right where I want him.

SPITEFUL CREATURES

And that's all it takes.

Intense pressure in all the perfect places combusts the energy that has edged within me for so damn long. It bursts like the flames of the sun as I convulse in their hands. Ryke's hold on my hair tightens as he has to hold me up, his hips slamming hard and fast with a grunt of noise joining my muffled screams, just as his hot slickness spurts over my tongue. I swallow it down fast at the back of my throat, and the pulsing of his cock against my tongue has a sensuous allure.

My lashes are still fluttering. My lips are swollen and my pussy is throbbing for more.

All those hands that were just providing me with the most pleasure of my entire life suddenly leave me, and I instantly feel cold and alone. Until the warmth of two palms takes my hips from behind and pulls me across the blankets like I'm a toy they're finally ready to play with.

"Head down," he whispers in a rumbling tone that shivers through me.

I peer back at him from over my shoulder and Zaviar's dangerously dark eyes meet mine.

"Head down," he commands once more.

He jerks my hips up high and I don't get to defy his instruction as my body bows for him of its own accord. My head touches the soft blankets and I inhale their warm sunshine scent. My heart taps a nervous beat of anticipation.

I wait for that delicious sinking feeling.

I wait.

And I wait.

I—fingers push through my hair and he forces my

throat back to a painful arch. My spine is curving toward him and it's my own sex that fucks him. Not the other way around. He uses my body to slide my wetness all down his shaft. He fills me entirely. With the hard pull of his hand in my hair, he eases the tension he's forcing into my position. A shaking breath slips from my lips as he grinds even deeper, rubbing and pushing as far as my walls will allow him.

The warmth of that demanding hand slips down from my hair to my neck and he holds me there firmly as he thrusts into me at a blurring pace that drills into me over and over and over again. The bite of his nails against my throat is an addicting sensation. It takes my breath away, but it takes my thoughts away even more.

Until…

"I was told you'd fuck whoever made you cum, love," a rasping voice says like the wind.

I nearly scream when I realize where that voice came from.

Zaviar doesn't halt his slapping thrusts.

Even with an incubus now lying lazily beneath me… between my thighs… and between Zaviar's knees.

The Seraph does not care. His grunt of pleasure isn't the least bit concerned by anything other than the drip of my pussy down his cock.

"A promise is a promise, Ari." His magic tinged fingers stroke along my jaw and open, gasping mouth.

His foot scrapes against my thigh and I feel the jarring effects of that little move as it collides with what must be Zaviar's hip.

"Fuck! Fuckin' demon spawn Hell prince!" Zav rants even more, but I'm oblivious to it as Krave shifts his body like a wave of motion and ever so slowly sinks into me like he never wants to leave.

And I hope he never does.

I can't help but moan from how deep his hardness kisses my womb.

The hold on me from behind turns more domineering from that small sound of my orgasmic appreciation.

"Fucking demons think they're some kind of gods damn gift to women," Zaviar growls.

"That's because we are." Krave replies, then the incubus rolls his hips so perfectly he slides against every part of my sex, my clit, and everywhere in between.

I cry out from the small movement that does oh, so much.

And it all just seems to piss Zaviar off even more.

He lifts me by my neck and then skims his palms down to my shoulders, positioning me on my knees over Krave. From the higher angle I can really see how pleased he is with himself.

Honestly, I am too at the moment.

Then from behind, something hard and throbbing brushes against the lower curve of my ass. The slickness of his tip glides down lower and lower. Until a pressure pushes just lightly against my sex… and Krave's cock.

"Relax, beautiful," Zaviar whispers to me, rubbing my shoulder in circular motions that make me forget the tense apprehension that's like molten iron dripping down my spine.

He grinds slow and deliciously there. The thought of what's to come turns those small thrusts into promises of pleasure. I arch against him, rocking into him as much as he rocks into me.

Krave stays ever so still, lips parted with soundless breath. It's the same breath I feel stuck in the back of my throat, so close. So, so close.

He slides right in. He slides in haltingly, grinding over every veiny inch of Krave's cock and stretching me to my fullest as the two of them fill me completely.

"Zaviar!" I beg. For what I don't know.

More.

More is what I want.

And he gives me just that.

The pounding of his body against mine is so hard that Krave's palms wrap around my waist. He supports me, he holds me up even as I start to lose myself in the euphoria that's consuming my mind, body, and soul.

My lashes flutter and I can only focus on the spiraling sensation building higher and higher and higher. It's an untouchable, neverending rise and fall. It lifts me up. It climbs. It soars.

But still it reaches no ceiling.

That is, until Krave's fingers slip slowly down the center of my chest. He trails down my body like he's making art of my form.

And maybe he is.

But the second his fingers slide down my folds, the rising spiral crashes. It comes down in flashing colors of blinding white bliss that tremble through me so hard I fold into Krave. The shaking of my scream is muffled into his neck while he strokes my hair, digging his fingers in and trying to worship me while groaning his own sounds of intoxication.

He fists my hair hard and I feel every muscle in his body convulse all at once as he throbs deep inside me.

And Zaviar still keeps going.

The jarring force of his hips tells me how close he is. Unfortunately, my own greedy release is well assembled all over again. And she's not waiting for him.

The waves that he drills through me are different this time. It's a static lashing that I feel all the way down to my toes. The clenching of my sex doesn't stop. I can't stop.

"Don't stop," I moan.

His response is a growl of groans and a cry he gives out signals more than he'll admit. But even if he did cum, he won't stop.

Not until I do.

My ass backs against him faster and faster. His grip there is so firm it hurts. In the best way possible.

It intensifies everything. Every. Single. Orgasmic. Wave.

When I cry out, with the voice crawling up my throat to express every desperation I have for these men, only then does he stop. Sweat clings to his chest and he holds me from behind. The weight of his temple rests along the back of my neck. Krave still caresses my hips, looking up at me like I'm the only goddess above he'll ever worship.

Zaviar slides away, falling to the mattress with a bounce and sigh, his hooded gaze holding mine while he toys with my fingers, not quite holding my hand.

"You look good when you're satisfied." He smiles slowly, wistfully.

"She so rarely is with you. Isn't that right?" Krave doesn't look at his friend, he simply continues to gaze up at me while Zaviar gives him a *I fucking loathe you* look.

"I hate you," Zaviar grunts before glancing away.

"Maybe so. But you can't unfuck me, now can you?"

Every nerve in Zaviar's body pricks up. He blinks a few times. And then shrugs his shoulders lightly.

I'm still smirking at them both when a warmth presses against me from behind. Ryke's beard tickles along my throat as he pulls me back against him. He brings me cross legged into his lap and I lean my head back on his hard chest to look up at his pretty eyes.

Steady fingers brush the hair from my sticky forehead as he looks adoringly at me. I lift my hips slightly against the outline pressing along my ass.

"Stop. This isn't a chore. Go to bed," he whispers.

Damien chuckles at his words and pulls me forward, towards the pillow that lies haphazardly at the top of the bed.

"Seriously, screwing four men sounds like too much to commit to." Damien still holds my hand, but I don't follow up to the pillow he wants so badly to put me to sleep in.

"Perhaps I should just be friends with some of you then."

Damien's eyebrows lift skeptically.

"Maybe you should. I hear Zaviar's shit in bed anyways. Some of us just aren't boyfriend material."

Damien swings his attention to his brother, but the mumbling annoyance from the Seraph shows he seems to be over the teasing for the night.

"Mate," I correct him like it's the most important thing. "You're my mates. Mine." I'm still hovering over Ryke while holding Damien's hand and all their attention is searing into me. "It isn't just the bond. It isn't just the unnerving way you four make me love you. And I fucking do. I love you," His eyebrows lift higher and I love the way he makes me feel as I say it again while I look back at Ryke, and then Zaviar who stands at the edge of the bed. And Krave who lies peacefully at the center. And then the sweetest half demon I've ever met. "It's the life we've shared. The realms we've fallen into for each other. We're mated because of our lives we've lived together. And we always will be," I whisper so lowly that my voice shakes at the thought of how deeply I love them.

Too deeply.

Damien steps forward at the end of the bed and he kisses me slowly, gently. His palm lines my jaw and it's the sweetest taste of intimacy.

Until I dip my head low and yank down his jeans.

He sways on his feet when my head lowers. With the heat of my breath teasing his tip, he curses something about chores. Then my lips part and I slide my mouth down him, one inch at time. The pulse that meets my tongue as I swirl against his cockhead is a rewarding stimulation that just demands that I give him more.

When I do it again, faster and faster, a drip of saltiness slides over my tongue as he groans out to the room. His hand slips through my hair and once I have his attention,

I demand anothers.

My back arches and I sway my hips, my wetness, my pussy.

Right. In. Front. Of Ryke's face.

I expect the rash of his beard against my thighs and sex.

But big hands brush up the curve of my ass. And then a thickness fills me fast and hard, jarring me into Damien as he thrusts into me like he won't wait for a single second longer. The grinding of his hips sinks into me at just the right angle. He rocks himself just right. It's like he's known every part of my body longer than I have.

He fucks me in a close, intimate way I never knew existed except in this moment between him and I. He leaves little room between us, not daring to leave that perfect spot within me for too long. He pounds into it again and again so it takes more from me in less time.

I feel him pulse deep inside me just before my own orgasm shatters. With slow deliberate thrusts, he drags out every ounce of sensual ecstasy in one big crash of chaotic pleasure that leaves me moaning and forgetful of the cock still waiting in my mouth.

As I groan around Damien he slides his hand down his member, gliding over himself fast and recklessly while his other hand holds my head in place. And it's these secret dominant displays he only shows me. It's the way he trusts me. It's the way he uses me.

It's everything sweet and sinful that defines him.

And it's the biggest fucking turn on as he uses my mouth for the thick, hot cum that slides down my throat, making me gag and gasp around him.

"Fuck, beautiful," he hisses as he jerks against my mouth.

The weakness of my limbs become apparent only when Ryke pulls me back against him for a second time. I collapse into his embrace, but I love the way he holds me. His warmth and gentleness surrounds me.

"Uh—Aries?" Someone says from outside the thick fog that's now covering my mind.

"Yeah?" I ask through the cloudy daze.

Krave motions a thumb toward the door.

"Your mom's room is right next to this one. Just thought you'd want to know."

With suddenly wide eyes I realize what he means.

This cottage isn't the biggest.

And my orgasms weren't the quietest.

Fuck.

CHAPTER FOURTEEN

FUCKED

Damien

We only sleep for an hour or so. She needs more rest than that. We all do.

But she's relentless. It's one of the many things I love about her.

"Come here," she motions to my brother as he drags a white shirt over his head, he's already following her command.

Like the whipped dog that he now is. I've never seen him care about anyone in his life.

Except for me.

Seeing him care about her the way I do, it seems to strengthen our bond. Despite how much the Bliss tries to break it.

Her gray eyes are so bright as she pulls out the spell book. Her long fingers loosen the thin leather noose that binds the front of it. Everyone watches in silence as she begins the most important moment of Zaviar's life.

She turns to the first page. The cream and tattered paper looks up at her. It's old, and the binding of the cover is weak, so it's to be expected that the first page is blank.

She shakes her head a bit, and flips to the next. I don't know where scholars or psycho demonic royals like Corva put their indexes, but it's not on the second page either. In fact, as Aries flips through the book, the first ten to twenty pages are all blank.

All of them are, actually.

"What the fuck!?" Aries frantically flips from front to back and then starts all over again.

"Is it under a spell? Invisible ink or something?" I ask, shifting closer to her in the already cramped bedroom.

"No… that's not it…." She throws the book with full force to the wall, its pages scattering on impact. "It's a fake!" Her jaw grinds and my heart falls as soon as she says it. "Corva planted a fake. And we're fucked."

Aries spins on her heels and she's storming out the door in a matter of seconds.

And I'm the last to react as the others chase after her.

Because as of now, my brother will be spending the rest of his fucking life in Realm Zero.

CHAPTER FIFTEEN
THE ATTACK
Aries

Putting their lives at risk for this spellbook was a stupid mistake. And I'm finished making mistakes.

I'm shoving open the cottage door when I come face to face with the kindest, most powerful woman in the Kingdom of Roses.

Or at least... she was once.

"You're going to confront her." My mother's big red wings are ruffling out in the morning sunlight. Her big eyes are innocent in a way that belies so much of the tragedy that has fallen around her over the years.

I'd thought a knowing motherly look would be in her gaze because of the orgasmic sounds that must have come from my room just earlier. That isn't there at all. Only concern shines through.

"I'm going to make things right." I try to walk past her, but her hand slides around my arm and there's a single moment of a childhood memory that gets jerked out of me.

A wanting, wanting to be praised and noticed by a woman who was too broken to even see the world around her, much less her own flailing daughter.

Her head tips down in thought before she meets my gaze earnestly.

"It terrified me that she was your only friend when you were little. It scared me to think you'd become something like her." Her voice is shallow and nearly cracking with emotion. "You're not, you know." My heartbeat stumbles. "You're nothing like Corva. Or your father. Or even me, really. You're incredible Aries. And I know you'll only do what's best for those you love."

Her hand slowly releases mine and her thin gown swooshes around her long legs as she passes the four men behind me. She walks inside and closes the door firmly but quietly,

She's wrong though.

I am like her. I'm a version of her who never got to exist because of my father's cruelty. It's funny how different our lives could have been if a single factor was changed. If my father were removed, my mother could have shaken kingdoms in her past. And if he were removed from my life, I wouldn't have the fire to burn them all down in my present.

My knees arch and I give no warning as I shove off from the ground, the wind catching my feathers. My hair tangles around my face before I shake it away and focus on the blueness of the sky, the softness of the clouds, and the nothingness in the distance ahead.

Four men with unyielding devotion soar around me like a protective halo prepared for the worst.

Because that is certainly what's to come.

The very worst.

* * *

We don't attack in the midst of the night as I would have when I was a young girl in the Shadow Guard.

My boots sound across the uneven cobblestones of my mother's beautiful rose garden, but I have no fond memories of childhood past as I stride up to the side entrance.

The cold metal of the door handle stings into my palm but before I pull it open, someone calls out to me.

"Princess," he enunciates my title in a proper accent and I remember the smart, political man from what feels like centuries ago.

"Johnn," I nod to him but now is not the time, Johnn. I'm a little busy here.

A goblin hobbles quickly along at his side.

Nille.

I eye the two of them and they both pass a look at the four men standing ready behind me. The cold wind lifts Johnn's light brown hair, and he looks tired. Years older than when we spoke in the meeting room just weeks ago.

"Your mother sent word that you'd be coming," Johnn says, catching his breath discreetly.

"How?" Ryke asks, echoing everyone's thoughts I'm sure.

Nille makes an aggressive disgruntled cough. As if we would ever doubt his abilities.

Which… I have no idea how he would have gotten a message here but as I said, now is not the time. My mother's sources reach far beyond conventional logic or even magic.

"You people whisper throughout this kingdom about the banished Princess's death. The Queen who never ruled." Johnn's words are rapidly spoken in the most ominous tone. "The Shadow Guard have not let them forget you. We're ready," he adds with a nod.

And then he opens the door for me, I walk through, and then he dashes off back the way he came.

"Weird bloke, that one." Krave tells Damien, and all four of them agree.

"Jealous much?" I ask as we creep through the quiet morning hall.

"Mmm of Johnn the accountant? No. Not at all."

"He's a Fae councilman."

"Yes, you see, I've had my encounters with councilmen. Not the best of folks, if you ask me."

"Shit, he is jealous," Damien whispers with a smirk kissing his words.

"Enough," Zaviar hisses just as we turn a corner.

A few castle staff members bustle around the large dining hall. Their black shoes click rapidly as they set the enormous table with silverware and fine china.

One very sullen girl in a bleak gray gown stares blankly at the scene swirling literally all around her motionless frame.

The thinness of her features and the dip of her royal bone structure makes her brown eyes seem enormous. Much larger than I remember.

"Penelopia," I say as inconspicuously as I can manage. I stride to her as if I've lived my life every day in this castle.

Instead of being cast out, killed, and reborn here.

It's been a happy little life, clearly.

Her head tips up to me, her gaze growing impossibly larger.

"She said you were coming. I didn't believe her." There's an emptiness ringing in her voice. A lostness that makes me wonder what she's endured here during my sister's short reign.

"Go for a walk, Pen." I touch her shoulder just lightly and even that feels too intimate for the nerves strumming through my body.

I want to tell her to run. Now! As fast as she can away from the hell that's about to land in this beautiful castle.

Instead, I nod to her. Her lifeless gaze stares back at me, her teal wings ruffling like a shiver. "She'll find you," she whispers. "She'll kill you for bringing the Bliss into her kingdom."

The Bliss...

"Who?" Ryke steps forward and the time they shared together flashes a single spark of relief across her features.

"Ryke." She steps closer to him as if the enormous morph demon can keep her safe.

Ryke can do a lot of things. Protect anyone he loves, but none of us are prepared for what we're walking into.

"Who's here, Pen?"

"The white demon. He arrived this morning with others." My cousin looks so young, but so wise all at the same

131

time. "You're the one who should leave, Aries. Because they're watching us. They're always watching."

A chill spider creeps down the back of my neck as her words ring out in my head.

They're watching us. They're watching us. They're watching us.

I peer around the bustle of the spacious dining room, looking up at the ceilings for the prying Pixies I'm so used to.

But no one of suspicion is here.

"Take a walk, Pen," I tell her once more, and then I head for the hall.

It's a roughly thought out plan of mine. I know my sister. I know she likes her own company above all others. And I know where I can find her.

When the five of us step foot into the seclusion of the small corridor, I turn to them.

"Krave, take Ryke to the top floor of the west wing."

"Your father's chambers?" Krave glances toward Ryke, but none of the men know the castle as well as Krave and myself.

"We'll be heading up the eastern wing and we'll meet just minutes apart in the bedchamber no one was allowed in."

Because it was Corva's. And everyone was too fucking afraid to go in there.

Krave nods.

"The three of us will enter first. We'll surprise her. And you two will attack her from behind moments later."

Zaviar also nods and when he looks at me, I feel a jolt of assurance in my half-cocked plan.

"Don't stop for anyone. If someone questions you,

keep going."

Krave slips his long fingers over the back of my hand, the way he looks at me unsettles the certainty I just had moments ago.

"I'll see you soon, love," he says like it's a secret meant only for us.

A tightness in my chest turns unbearable when he leads Ryke away. I want to call out to them. To change my mind about all of this and take them back to that pretty mansion in the Bin and hide away there for the rest of our beautiful lives together.

But there's not time for that. We're too far into this. And too many people are counting on us now for us to just fall back into selfish thoughts.

Zaviar and Damien match my pace as I lead us down the dark halls and through the big entryway that opens up with bright sunlight and far more people than I anticipated.

Johnn stands at the center of the room and though a few people pass us glances, his gaze catches mine. He never once stutters as he continues the morning agenda to the staffer.

"The Queen will not dispose of you. That is not her intent."

He's good at saying the right things under distress.

Almost.

"Like she did my son? Like she did the King? Like she did Princess Aries?" A guard calls out from the back.

I lower my head even more, shaking my hair out to glamour my features into an elder woman in black staff attire. The magic tingles through my flesh, creating wrinkles along my face and hands, with graying feathers here and there throughout my wings.

"I hate when you do that," Zaviar whispers in a disturbed tone.

"You'd rather I get us caught instead?"

"No, I'd rather you give a bit of warning before you turn my sexy fuckin' mate into Great Grandma Edith."

I continue trailing up the stairs at a rather fast pace for someone with Grandma Edith's appearance but who knows, maybe she's a big fan of jazzercise.

Or maybe she's got a Queen to kill.

We turn down the first floor and the next stairwell is just to the left. But a guard stands at the center there, his back turned to us for a brief moment.

My breath free-falls in my lungs as I shove the two men behind me back down the stairs, hearing them stumble just slightly out of sight.

And then a new glamour casts over my flesh, prickling and biting into transformation. Inky locks cascade down my shoulders and the ghostly sensation of my very being flickers through me in a painful way.

It's unnatural for a Fae to take this form.

Almost as unnatural as she is.

"My Queen," the man kneels so low his knee literally hits the floor.

It isn't a stance of loyalty or respect.

It's fear.

"You. What was your name?" I point a thin finger at him and the man visibly shivers in his smooth black uniform as he stands back up to address me... Corva... us.

"Brentin. You said just yesterday I was your favorite guard…" That fear shines brighter in his eyes.

Fuck, what has Corva been doing to these people?

"Yes. Well. I lied, Brentin." When the sneer of my words greets him, panic lines his brow. "I'm rather displeased with your services. I'd like you to take some time off. Go home for the day." My arms fold across my black satin gown like the bad bitch that I am.

"Does that mean… you don't want to fuck me anymore too?"

A burning hot gag stings the back of my throat.

"Yes. That's what that means, Brentin. I said I was displeased with your *services*. Now go home!"

Get the fuck away from this nightmare that's about to come to life, Brentin.

He quickly takes off, stumbling on his feet as he passes me. When he rushes down the stairs, he doesn't utter a word to Zaviar or Damien.

The two of them walk up to me rather hesitantly.

"He didn't even glance our way," Damien says.

"That's because his vision was blurred by the fuckin' tears in his eyes. You should be nicer, beautiful." Zaviar strides up the small stairwell first.

"I need as many people out of this place as I can."

"And you have to embarrass their manhood along the way?"

I think it over…

I suppose there are kinder ways. But that doesn't fit Corva's character at the moment. No one speaks again for several moments while we carefully make our way to the top of the castle, stopping just shy of the tower.

My prickling glamour fades away while I look down to the opposite end of the corridor.

They're not here yet.

Perfect.

I stare into the deep lines of grain etching the old wooden door. The inhale that reaches my lungs is a shaky breath, but it's all I allow myself. I can't overthink this moment.

I can only react.

My wrist turns against the handle. The hinges scream out as the heavy door glides over the wooden floor and she doesn't look up at me when I ambush her.

It's so much of an under-reaction from my sister that I slow my running steps when I'm in the middle of the small room and truly assess my surroundings.

It feels like a trap.

She sits with slumped posture in the worn wooden chair with her head hung low, her hair veiling around her pale face and I almost wonder if she's sleeping…

The glossy black locks around her face shift just minimally. They wave around her slender neck, moving ever so slightly around her head. Until it slides right off her shoulders.

And tumbles to the floor with a rolling thud that only stops when her chin hits my boot.

My lips part. A scream that I refuse to release catches in my throat. The only sound is the knocking of my heart in my ears and I feel frozen to the spot as I stare down at her severed head.

Warm fingers wrap around my wrist. A familiar voice whispers something to me, but the sound is muted. Everything feels detached.

Especially the blade that nicks my shoulder just before I'm shoved away. I stumble over something, my boot rolling over the thing as I catch my balance against the wall and look up in time to see Zaviar catching a blade in his bare hands and shoving the person back.

The man staggers, but he's right back in place within half a second. His blade that he raises high above his head shimmers like the sun. It comes down with a hard arch and Zaviar barely sidesteps the blow.

Damien's on top of another man, his fist pummeling down over and over again, but all I see is the blood there before a blinding light swings out at me. My wings flare out as I kick off to the left, barely missing the blade that's now pointed at me.

When I land once more, I find the white demon Darien smiling widely at me. More Seraphs fill the room, dozens of them pressing in on us as I stare up at the spiraling colorless horns atop his head.

He holds his Bliss blade loosely in his right hand. Clearly, not invested in using it while we're so very outnumbered.

I catch sight of a small woman standing outside the bedroom door and it surprises me to see the unease in Mira's face.

"This isn't our domain. And we're not approved to be here. You said we'd be in and out, Darine." She's the good one after all. And she clearly doesn't approve of the ambush happening here in the Fae realm.

He ignores her.

I bet he does that a lot.

"I told Corva to bring me my Seraph." He turns his attention to my thrashing mate who's being held down by three white winged men. And then he rears his hoof back and flings it forward against the angle of Zaviar's jaw.

I lunge for him. My feet shove off the old floorboards so hard I hear a crack sound out. The force that I sink my nails into the back of his neck with is a bleeding press that bites right through his flesh.

His arm comes down hard and the weight of his mysterious sword alone knocks into my skull as I'm slammed to the floor. My shoulder throbs, but the blood on his shoe— Zaviar's blood—and it motivates me.

My leg kicks up high, slinging out and catching at the back of his knee. He hits the ground and rolls in the blink of an eye.

He's on top of me in less than a breathless second.

His thin hands lock around my biceps.

"All three of you are coming to Realm Zero. I'm going to finish what we started, pretty princess," his thick breath washes over my lips from his closeness.

My knee comes up hard, but at the last second someone stomps on my shin. Pain radiates right through the bone.

"Fuck!" I cry out with a scream.

The sound of my misery is a weakness I hate to admit to.

But it sounds an alarm of sorts. It seems to alert the army within this fortress.

The room is quiet for a beat.

A buzz generates slowly. It grows and grows into a

dark growl of a sound.

And then Krave speaks.

"There he is, Pixies. That's the mother fucker who killed your Queen," Krave's amused tone is cut short by the sound of a hive of Pixies flurrying into the room like fiery falling stars looking to end an era.

The beat of their rapid wings is a war cry that carries on as they attack the Seraphs, Darine in particular.

My mates join them as thrashing violence thunders through the room. I claw at the man who seems relentless in releasing my arms.

"We're leaving!" he announces.

"The fuck you are," I answer.

And with the help of a thousand angry little Pixies, I slide my foot beneath me and kick off from the ground, holding his hands against me. His grip eases as his icy eyes widen and still I cling to him. Little wings help carry his weight and I thrust my way through the overcrowded space. We spill out into the darkness of the hall.

"Let go of me!" His long nails claw into my wrists, but still I hold him tightly in my hands.

"If I kill you," my wings beat hard, "you'll just reform in the Bliss." Faster I fly us away from the noise of the chaotic room filled with too much blood.

"I said unhand me!" He grips tightly at my throat now, but the determination will never settle in me.

Not when it comes to this angelic fuck.

A tightness constricts against my lungs. It burns as I choke against it. And still I fly.

His knuckles turn white. A dry gasp stutters from my

lips and his eyes light up. Nails sink into my flesh. I dip down against the stairs as I lose my balance. But still I fly.

The cool wind of the tower tossels my hair. It's a beautiful sunny morning. Light beams into the glorious castle my ancestors built. Magic of my own and magic of another twirls together within my blood.

I channel that sensation as I drag Darien to the edge of the tower. He kicks at me. He holds harder against my windpipe. The force of it blurs my vision, but I can clearly see the way the sun kisses the red roses far down below.

They're an image of untouched perfection. The haunting image of my brother's bloody face flashes through my mind.

So much death surrounds those flowers. Maybe someday my own will as well.

Maybe… maybe… maybe…

I step off the ledge.

I hold him close, like he's the only person I care about in all the realms. And in this moment, he is.

"I hope you enjoyed what you did to my mate." I whisper so lowly that it gets caught up in the lashing of the wind. My lashes flutter closed as I embrace my demons. I accept the darkness that I'm made of. I hold on to what's left of Catherine and all that she's given me.

And then… everything goes black.

CHAPTER SIXTEEN
A WARM WELCOMING
Aries

Seeing the fear in his eyes when his pale lashes finally open is the most rewarding gift.

Sand shifts beneath his dusty hooves as he tries to stand on the unforgiving ground. The heat here will be the worst for him. That comb over will not make it one fucking day.

"Where… where are we?" he turns, kicking up sand as he fully takes in his surroundings.

I made sure the city was a far off walk for him. And even when he gets there… they won't take kindly to someone like him.

"Welcome to the Torch, Councilman."

My arms span wide as I give him the grand tour of… the sand. It's everywhere. And really, it's all he's going to be coming across for days.

Unless a demon finds him first.

"How did you get here? Fae and Seraph cannot channel to the Torch!" He shakes his head adamantly.

He thinks I'm bluffing.

I'm fucking not.

"That's true. But I'm not just a Fae." I shove a gentle hand against his shoulder and his feet stumble over the sliding ground and I have to kneel down when he lands on his ass. "Here's a little tip. Don't ever threaten Fae royalty. And don't fucking threaten a demon Fae!"

I stand, and the powerful magic of an amazing Queen mingles with my own. I'm already leaving before I've said my goodbye.

That would be rude. We can't do that…

"Enjoy your stay in Hell, Dar."

His scream follows after me. It echoes in my head even after I've left. I marinate in the happiness it brings to me as I step into the yelling match that has descended in the room my sister lived and died in.

"I want you to leave," I say flatly to Mira.

Damien looks up at me with dried blood staining his upper lip and silence follows my words.

The Seraphs are much fewer now. Only three of them stand with Mira. She's composed. Not a hair is out of place on her head and it eases my mind to know she wasn't hurt in all of this.

"We're leaving. I assure you. Where's Darine?" She

looks me up and down.

The claw marks at my throat sting and the dryness of my lips from the heat of the Torch hurts when I swallow slowly.

"I said I want you to leave." I look her dead in the eyes and she shifts on her white heels.

"I understand," she says curtly.

She motions to the Seraphs, but I halt her before she moves another inch.

"Zaviar's bond with your kind is null." I hold my head high and she peers over at the man in question. "He's a Seraph and he's bound to Demon Fae. He'll never be able to uphold your laws. No matter how much of an angel boy my sweet mate may be."

Ryke's rumbling laughter is quieted as a thudding sound seems to hit him square in the stomach.

Mira looks away. Her gaze slips to the bright light beaming into the tiny room as if she's seeking the sun gods' advice.

"I'll never let him go," I add for good measure. "And you and I both know I have the resources to bring him back to me time and time again."

Her eyes close slowly.

"I'll file discharge paperwork this afternoon." She looks up at me with a swift turn of her head.

One by one the white winged men trail after their councilwoman. They're quieter on their way out than they were on their way in.

Assholes.

I'm still silently glaring at the most monstrous

creatures I've ever met as they walk away.

With aching pain bruising into every part of my body, I can't help but wonder how Zaviar is anything like them.

I guess it's because he's not.

He's mine.

They all are.

EPILOGUE

Krave

There's a magic in scars. They tell a story of a time long ago. The scars the five of us carry, they're more than magic.

They speak of unimaginable pain, but also of unbreakable love. We all wear them. The white shining lines are a history of what we've been through together.

Aries' soft hand slips into mine with ease as she smiles up at me like she never once held hate in her heart for me. Like I wasn't a traitor to her for all those years.

She simply looks at me like I'm one of four men who know her inside and out.

Her attention spans the meeting room--the *war room* as

her father once called it. It has since been renamed The Room of Conference.

As it should be.

Her full lips move as she answers another of Johnn's dull political questions.

"Well, the expanse to the East is all flatlands," Damien inserts. Literally inserts. Poor bastard is out observing and measuring grass in his free time because that's what Aries asked of him.

Ryke kisses the side of her head just near her pretty horns and she beams from the small contact as he heads to the door to review said expanse.

It's. Flat. Land.

What more is there to survey?

"Zaviar, will you go with him? See if our village can extend more to the North as well."

"Of course," Zaviar sends her a long and lingering look from across the room that makes her cheeks tinge just slightly pink.

Whipped. All of them.

They've all been busy since the moment Ari freed and welcomed demons into her kingdom. Something that's never once happened in all the years I remember.

I yawn quietly and wait for the meeting to come to an end, my hand twirling an image of a flat land… and how perfect it'd be to toss a certain beautiful demon Fae down on that expanse and explore her expanse…

"Krave," she whispers, her thumb brushing back and forth against my knuckles in a hypnotic way.

I perk up immediately. She says my name like a rasp of

pleasure. My dick hardens for the third time during today's meeting.

"Would you draw up a city plan this evening, take the measurements of the North and Eastern flatlands from Ryke and Zav and see what we can do for the misplaced demons in our realm?"

"I can do that, my love."

"Yeah? I know you've already made twenty-seven this week, but I'm really hoping this location will work for the housing of our newly welcomed people."

"Yes. Definitely. What's one more, darling?"

One more. Twenty-eight more. Nine hundred. It takes no time at all. And the reaction she gives me each and every time makes it all worth it. Fuck let me go draw it up right now.

Her smile radiates. It burns right into my fluttering heart like the whipped fuck puppy I'm lucky enough to be.

And what a delicious pride it is to be so loved by a woman so utterly selfless. She once cherished an incubus more than she did her own cruel father.

And I think that's what gave her that new shining crown that sits atop her pretty silver hair.

That's what gave her her title: The *Queen* of Roses, Traveler of Realms, Empress of Peace.

Aries Sinclair.

My fucking beautiful mate.

THE END.

SPITEFUL CREATURES

Thank you so much for reading the series with some of my favorite characters! If you're looking for more badass Fae women and epic romance, check out my completed series, The Hopeless Series!

Turn the page for a preview of book one, _Hopeless Magic_.

HOPELESS MAGIC

Coarse strands of rope twist through my fingers as I haul myself even higher up the tower. My fingers thread right through it and I realize the rope hanging from the window isn't a rope at all but … human hair.

The night wind whips cruelly against me, pushing my small frame against the side of the disintegrating brick wall. My pale locks sting across my cheeks. I clench my jaw and lift my gaze higher to the window with the blinking light. It's unnatural. The white light burns brightly into the dark sky before fading into nothingness.

I heave another breath as my boots shift against the wall and I pull myself up the ancient tower. Rocks scrape and crumble beneath my every move, falling away with ease. A stinging numbness sets into my thin fingers and I'm starting to wish I had stolen that drunk's coat before I left the bar.

The way he spoke about the unseen tower miles out of town, the tales he told of the wealth that rests within it, had my feet moving before he'd even slurred a word of warning.

No one's ever been able to warn me of anything, though. So what if I'm an orphan? So what if I'm not tall enough or strong enough? So what if I'm a girl? So what if I'm too pretty to be taken seriously?

That's never stopped me before, and it certainly isn't going to stop me from claiming the prize at the top of this fortress.

Solid brick greets my nails as I dig into the opening of the window. A burning breath stings my lungs. I throw my leg over the ledge and slip inside without a sound.

The light's gone now. Darkness veils my sight. The long hair that leads me up the tower is tied off on a rusting hook. Next to the hook is something white. Something familiar. Something that makes my skin crawl just looking at it.

A human skull.

I turn away, rejecting the sight of it. My shoulders square and I pull the sword from my belt. The weight of it settles my nerves. It was my father's. Before I was a thief, I was just a pretty little girl with a promising future ahead of her. After my father's death was when I learned all the things that made me the resilient woman I am today.

His blade helped mold me even without his presence.

Something in the shadows shifts, my gaze sweeps every inch of the dark room.

"You should leave. Now," a deep voice warns. But he's too late.

A short dagger glints in the moonlight. I barely have

time to see the shine of it before it quickly sinks into my side.

Horrified gasps part my lips and my brows pull together in anger and confusion.

The attacker slips the dagger from my flesh as quickly as it came. My fingers slide slickly across my skin as I press hard against the wound.

Hot blood pools through my fingertips. My heart thrashes in my chest and I just know.

It's fatal.

Painfully, my jaw clenches as a scarred and twisting face reveals itself to me.

"You should have listened to our little Prince, love." His gruff voice crawls through the small room. Shadows hide his features from me, but he tilts his head to the corner of the room at the mention of *our little Prince*.

I breathe hard before raising my father's sword with more strength than I intend. I plunge it into the man, railing it through his abdomen. I don't stop until it's all the way through his wide body, clinking against the brick wall behind him.

His glossy eyes hold mine, and my lips purse firmly as I hold his stare.

It's a look that screams *fuck off.* It's a look I usually reserve for clingy boyfriends, but I suppose it works here as well.

Even as I bleed out, I'll cling to that false sense of strength I always seem to hold.

I don't have the energy to retrieve the blade from his frame as he sinks to the floor with a solid thud. My vision blurs, my breaths becoming shorter and shorter. It's an effort just to take shallow gasps of air.

I've seen death enter a man's eyes before with a vacant and fearful shine. I've seen his life slip through his fingertips.

It won't be long now …

"Get the key," someone whispers. His voice circles the room.

As I stand here dying someone seems to think they have something more important to be doing. My death seems to really be interfering with their fabulous day.

The white light I saw from the woods, the white light that lead me here to my death, it strikes through the room once more. It flickers sporadically, waning into a dim hue of gold.

Three men stand gripping the bars of a jail cell in the corner of the room. The one with golden hair holds his hands together as if he's harnessing a force between his palms. The light burns with a pulsing hue from the center of his hands.

What is he holding?

"Come on, we've been here for over a year, love. Get the key."

A shaking breath filled with annoyance parts my dry lips.

"Did you see what happened to the last man that called me *love*?" I narrow my eyes on the prisoner with the pale gray gaze. My lips twist with confidence even though I feel my strength fading.

The other man at his side turns to him with a smirk pulling at his features. There's a similarity between the two men. One holds taunting humor and the other total anger. It's then that I realize they're the same.

They're twins.

"Please, lo—*woman*, get the key." Yes, because women

love nothing more than to be called affectionately by their gender.

Asshole.

The scowl never leaves his handsome, dirty face as he points across the room to a single key displayed proudly in a glass case. A dim light illuminates the key, taunting them with the closeness of their freedom.

The scraping sound of my boots moving sluggishly skims through the small room. I lean into the wall as I reach high for the brass key.

The thin display case teeters and the enclosing box falls away from the key. Fine particles of glass shatter across my boots but I don't notice it as I stand on the tips of my toes to reach the key. It's cold against my skin. My fingerless leather gloves are all that separates its metal from my numbing flesh.

I turn back to them and the three stand wide-eyed, watching me with expectation as I hold their lives in my hands.

Over the years, I've been taught to never give anything away for free. A person's life is worth quite a bit.

I know because mine's already gone.

Panic wraps itself tightly around my stomach as I realize I can't manage a real intake of air. I push aside the selfish thought and walk to them with fear gripping my chest. My life is over, but their lives don't have to be. The key fits perfectly into the lock with a scraping sound of metal on metal. It turns with ease.

One of the twins claps his hands as they all race from the cell.

My eyes close heavily and I sink to the floor in a warm puddle of my own blood. Slick fingers fall from the fatal puncture wound, my hands no longer able to hold the life within me.

The man with dark hair, one of the twins, lowers himself down to his knees. Crimson blood stains his dirty jeans.

He clings tightly to a mysterious light in his hands.

"Thank you," he says. My eyes flutter, wanting to see him—the last person who will ever see me before I die.

I guess I won't die alone after all.

The effort of opening my eyes is too much.

He presses a warm kiss to my temple. It's an affectionate gesture that I would have hated if I weren't teetering on the hazy line between life and death. It feels nice, though. To feel loved. To feel treasured. To feel … like my life mattered.

Even if it is just pretend.

A painful, empty breath shakes from my lungs, the last one I have the strength to take.

Heat radiates through my side as he presses his hand to my flesh, just over the knife wound. A light shines brightly against my closed lids. Nerves tingle all through my body.

A strong sound pounds loudly through my ears, filling my hazy consciousness.

My heartbeat.

Order *Hopeless Magic* today!

ALSO BY A.K. KOONCE

REVERSE HAREM BOOKS

The To Tame a Shifter Series

Taming

Claiming

Maiming

Sustaining

Reigning

The Villainous Wonderland Series

Into the Madness

Within the Wonder

Under the Lies

Origins of the Six

Academy of Six

Control of Five

Destruction of Two

Wrath of One

The Hopeless Series

Hopeless Magic

Hopeless Kingdom

Hopeless Realm

Hopeless Sacrifice

A.K. KOONCE

The Secrets of Shifters

The Darkest Wolves

The Sweetest Lies

The Royal Harem Series

The Hundred Year Curse

The Curse of the Sea

The Legend of the Cursed Princess

The Severed Souls Series

Darkness Rising

Darkness Consuming

Darkness Colliding

The Huntress Series

An Assassin's Death

An Assassin's Deception

An Assassin's Destiny

Dr. Hyde's Prison for the Rare

Escaping Hallow Hill Academy

Surviving Hallow Hill Academy

PARANORMAL ROMANCE BOOKS

The Cursed Kingdoms Series

The Cruel Fae King

SPITEFUL CREATURES

The Cursed Fae King

The Crowned Fae Queen

The Twisted Crown Series

The Shadow Fae

The Iron Fae

The Midnight Monsters Series

Fate of the Hybrid, Prequel

To Save a Vampire, Book one

To Love a Vampire, Book two

To Kill a Vampire, Book three

STAND ALONE CONTEMPORARY ROMANCE

Hate Me Like You Do

Printed in Great Britain
by Amazon